NIGHT OF THE
GIANT EVERYTHING

GOOSEBUMPS HorrorLand™

Also Available from Scholastic Audio Books

GOOSEBUMPS®
HALL OF HORRORS

NIGHT OF THE GIANT EVERYTHING

R.L. STINE

SCHOLASTIC INC.
New York Toronto London Auckland
Sydney Mexico City New Delhi Hong Kong

No part of this publication may be reproduced, stored in a retrieval system, or transmitted in any form or by any means, electronic, mechanical, photocopying, recording, or otherwise, without written permission of the publisher. For information regarding permission, write to Scholastic Inc., Attention: Permissions Department, 557 Broadway, New York, NY 10012.

ISBN: 978-0-545-28935-1

Goosebumps book series created by Parachute Press, Inc.
Copyright © 2011 by Scholastic Inc.

12 11 10 9 8 7 6 5 4 3 2   11 12 13 14 15 16/0

Printed in the U.S.A.   40
First printing, May 2011

WELCOME TO THE HALL OF HORRORS

THERE'S ALWAYS ROOM FOR ONE MORE SCREAM

Before you enter, please wipe your shoes on the KEEP OUT mat. We try to keep the floors clean. The housecreeper hasn't cleaned for a while. You'll have to forgive the BLOODSTAINS.

Yes, you've found my old castle, a place for very special visitors only. This is a place for kids who have stories to tell.

Come sit by the fire. Don't you like the way the flames leap to the ceiling? Too bad we don't have a fireplace.

I am the Story-Keeper. Here in the darkest, most hidden part of HorrorLand, I keep the doors to the Hall of Horrors open.

Frightened kids find their way here. Haunted kids. They are eager to tell me their stories. I am the Listener. And I am the Keeper of their tales.

Those shadowy faces on the wall? The faces with bulging eyes and mouths open in screams of horror? Those are paintings of the kids who brought their stories to me.

We have a visitor today. That boy sitting in the armchair by the fire. He's nervously juggling three red balls in the air.

His name is Steven Sweeney. Steven is twelve, and he's into magic and illusions. But what happened to him was no illusion.

"What is your story about, Steven?"

"It's about . . . dangerous magic."

"You enjoy performing tricks, don't you?"

"Tricks can be fun. What happened to me was horrifying!"

"Well, go ahead, Steven. I am the Story-Keeper. Start at the beginning. Tell me your story."

Steven lets the three red balls fall to his lap. His dark eyes burn into mine. "Are you sure? It's a very weird story," he says.

Go ahead, Steven. Don't be afraid. There's Always Room for One More Scream in the HALL OF HORRORS. . . .

"Pick a card. Any card."

I held the deck up to Ava and Courtney. They're in my class. Ava Munroe and Courtney Jackson.

They both laughed. "Steven, we know this trick," Ava said.

Ava is the tallest girl in the sixth grade at Everest Middle School. She's very pretty, with wavy blond hair and blue eyes. But I think being so tall gives her an attitude.

She likes to look down on me. And I'm only two or three inches shorter than she is.

I waved the deck of cards in their faces. "Maybe this trick is different. Go ahead. Pick one and don't tell me what it is."

Courtney crossed her arms in front of her blue hoodie. "It's the ace of hearts," she said without picking a card.

Courtney is African American, with short hair and big dark brown eyes. She wears long, dangling earrings and lots of beads. She has a great laugh.

I hear her laugh a lot. Because she likes to laugh at me and my magic tricks.

"How do you know your card will be the ace of hearts?" I asked.

"Because every card in the deck is the ace of hearts," Courtney replied.

She and Ava bumped knuckles and laughed again.

"Okay, okay," I said. "You guessed that one." I tucked the trick deck of cards into my jacket pocket. "But here's a trick you don't know. Can you spare any change?"

I reached up and pulled a quarter from Ava's nose.

Ava groaned. "Steven, that's totally obnoxious. Why are you always doing that?"

Obnoxious is one of her favorite words. Her brother is obnoxious. Her dog is obnoxious. Today she said her *lunch* was obnoxious. I'm not kidding.

"I just feel a change in the air," I said. I pulled a quarter from Courtney's ear. I spun it in my fingers and made it disappear.

"Know where the quarter went?" I asked. "Ava, open your mouth."

"No way," she said, spinning away from me.

"Steven, give us a break," Courtney said. "We've seen all your tricks—remember?"

4

It was a cool fall day. A gust of wind blew my hair over my eyes. I have long, straight black hair. My mom calls it a *mop* of hair. She likes to wait till I brush it just right and then mess it up with both hands.

Everyone in my family is funny.

Most of the guys in my class have very short hair. But I like it long. It's more dramatic when I'm doing my comedy magic act onstage.

Ava, Courtney, and I were standing at the curb on Everest Street. School had just let out. Kids were still hurrying out of the building. The wind swirled, sending brown leaves dancing down the street.

Courtney tucked her hands into her hoodie. "So tomorrow is the talent assembly?"

I nodded. "Yeah. My act is going to *kill*."

"Not if Courtney and I kill you first!" Ava said.

Ha-ha. LOL. They're both crazy about me. Otherwise, they wouldn't say things like that—right?

"You're my assistants tomorrow. Remember?" I said. "We have to rehearse the act. Practice your moves."

Courtney squinted at me. "You're not going to pull quarters out of our noses in front of the whole school, are you?"

"Do you have any tricks that aren't obnoxious?" Ava asked.

"For sure," I said. "Here. Check out this new trick."

They didn't see the spray can of Silly String hidden at my side.

I leaned forward. Then I pretended to sneeze on Ava. A biiig sneeze.

And as I sneezed, I squirted a stream of white Silly String all over the front of her sweater.

She gasped and staggered back in surprise.

It was a riot.

But then Courtney tried to grab the Silly String can from my hand.

And that's when things went out of control.

Courtney swiped at the can. My finger pushed down on the button. And squirted the stuff all over her face and in her hair.

"Yuck!" She let out a cry and tried to wipe the Silly String gunk from her eyes.

Then Ava grabbed the can and sprayed it on me. I couldn't squirm away. She kept her finger down on the top and covered me in a ton of the sticky stuff. Then she tossed the can to the curb.

I started slapping at the stuff. Trying to pull it off my jacket. Courtney was still rubbing her eyes, smearing it off her cheeks. A big gob was stuck to her hair.

"Steven, do you know how to spell *revenge*?" she asked through gritted teeth.

"Do you know how to spell *joke*?" I shot back.

Kids were laughing and cheering. One kid from the third grade picked up the can from the ground and tried to squirt his friend. But the can was empty.

"Steven, you creep. You ruined my sweater!" Ava cried.

"It comes out," I said. "The can says it's washable. It was just a joke, Ava."

"*You're* a joke!" she cried angrily. She tried to punch me in the gut, but I danced away. I'm smaller and faster.

I glanced at my phone and saw the time. "I'm late for my piano lesson," I said.

I started across the street. But then I turned back and called to Ava. "I'll come to your house after my lesson, and the three of us can rehearse the magic act."

"Not if I see you first!" she shouted.

Courtney waved both fists at me.

I told you. They're crazy about me.

Mr. Pinker is my new piano teacher. He gives lessons from his house, which is just two blocks from the school.

He has a big redbrick house that sits on top of a wide grassy yard that tilts sharply downhill. In the winter, he lets the neighborhood kids use the hill for sledding.

The house is old, with ivy crawling up one wall. It has two chimneys and a long screened-in porch.

I climbed the hill to his house. Rang the bell and let myself in the front door.

The front hall was brightly lit, cluttered with coats and caps and umbrellas hanging on hooks. I could hear piano music from the front room. Someone was finishing a lesson. The house smelled of fresh-baked cookies.

I set down my backpack and tossed my jacket onto one of the hooks. A short red-haired girl gave me a smile as she headed out the front door.

"Hello, Steven. Come in," Mr. Pinker greeted me. "That was Lisa. She got the piano keys all warmed up for you."

He seems like a nice guy. I guess he's about forty or so. He's tall and thin. Mostly bald, with a fringe of red-brown hair around his head. He wears glasses low on his nose.

He always wears a gray suit and a red necktie. This was only my third lesson with him. He's worn the same outfit each time.

I followed him into the front room. It was kind of old-fashioned. Lots of old chairs and a big brown leather couch with the leather peeling off in places. A tall grandfather clock on the far wall had the minute hand missing. It didn't work.

Four black-and-white photographs of sailboats hung on one wall. A painting of a symphony conductor with his baton raised stood over the mantel.

A low desk in one corner had stacks and stacks of sheet music on it. The piano stood against the other wall, facing the front window. A window seat also held tall stacks of piano sheet music.

Outside, the gusting wind sent a tree branch tapping the front window. It sounded like drumbeats.

"What's that white stuff in your hair?" Mr. Pinker asked. "Are you getting dandruff?"

I reached up. My hair was sticky. "It's Silly String," I said. "I had a little Silly String battle."

He nodded. "Make sure your fingers aren't sticky." Then he disappeared from the room.

A few seconds later, he returned with a big home-baked chocolate chip cookie on a plate and a glass of milk. "I know sixth-graders are hungry after school," he said. "That's why I bake my special cookies for my students every day."

He handed me the plate and set the glass of milk down on a coaster on the piano. I wasn't really hungry, but I didn't want to be rude. I took a big bite of the cookie.

It was very chewy and a gob of it stuck to the roof of my mouth. I tried to wash it down with a sip of milk.

Mr. Pinker pushed the plate under my nose. "Go ahead. Finish it, Steven. All the kids enjoy them."

I forced the cookie down, sipping milk after every bite.

As Mr. Pinker watched me eat, he got this big smile on his face. His eyes lit up and he kept grinning. He watched till I finished every last crumb.

But there was nothing *strange* about that— right?

"This is one of Chopin's early pieces," Mr. Pinker said. He set the sheet music down on the piano. "I think you will find it easy to play, once you get used to the rhythm."

"I practiced the other piece you gave me last week," I told him. "But I only have a small keyboard at home, so it's hard to do it right."

Mr. Pinker patted my shoulder. "Once your parents hear how good you are, they will want to buy you a real piano," he said.

I guess I am pretty good at it. I'm not bragging. Music comes pretty easily for me. Same with magic and doing stand-up comedy and other stuff onstage. I just like to perform.

Dad says my uncle David sang and played piano with a very popular dance band. He died before I was born. But maybe I get my talent from him.

I pulled the piano bench up closer and leaned over the music. I tried to figure out the fingering of the first few bars.

Mr. Pinker was wrong. This piece was hard. Very fast and complicated. I knew it would take hours of practice to get my fingers moving fast enough.

Mr. Pinker slid next to me on the piano bench. "Let's try a few measures," he said. "I'll show you."

I still had the chocolate taste in my mouth. Mr. Pinker's cookie was so rich, my stomach was already churning.

I watched his hands as he started to play. I kept moving my eyes from his hands up to the music. Then I tried the first few bars . . . very slowly.

We worked on the piece together for about twenty minutes. It was pretty intense. But I was starting to get it right.

The phone interrupted us. Mr. Pinker jumped to his feet and started for the kitchen. "I have to answer that," he said. "Keep practicing the first few pages."

I leaned forward and moved my fingers over the keys. My hands were sweaty. I dried them off on the towel Mr. Pinker keeps on the piano.

My back ached. I hadn't moved in nearly half an hour. I decided to stand up and stretch.

Where was the bathroom? This would be a good time to go. But I'd never seen the rest of the house.

The kitchen was to the left. To the right, I saw a long hallway. I decided there must be a bathroom down there.

I stepped into the hall. There were no lights on. But I could see doors on both sides. The floor was wood and creaked under my shoes. The air smelled like pine, like bathroom cleaner or something.

My eyes adjusted to the dim light. I could see that the doors along the hall were all closed.

I pulled open the first door and peered inside. It was a closet with sheets and towels piled on the shelves.

I closed that door and walked to the next door. It was partway open. I peeked inside and saw a twin bed and a dresser. Probably a guest bedroom.

Maybe I should have waited and asked Mr. Pinker where the bathroom was. But there *had* to be one in this long hall, I figured.

My shoes made the floor creak and squeak. I stepped up to the next door and pulled it open. Gazing inside, I blinked several times—and let out a startled gasp.

Gray afternoon light poured in from two windows on the far wall. I gripped the doorknob and stared down at the floor.

What was I seeing? A tiny town? A tiny town of wooden dollhouses?

Before my eyes could focus, Mr. Pinker's angry scream rang through the hall. "Get OUT of there! SHUT that door! GET AWAY! Right NOW!"

I jumped a mile. And pulled the door shut.

"Steven!" Mr. Pinker cried. "What are you *doing* there?"

"Well—I—uh—" I stammered. "I'm sorry. I was looking for a bathroom, Mr. Pinker."

"The bathroom is at the end of the hall," he said. He pointed. He still had an angry look on his face.

I was shaking a little. I mean, I didn't understand why he was so angry.

What was in that room? Why was it such a big secret?

A little while later, I came back to the living room. He was seated on the piano bench. He had a thoughtful look on his face.

I wanted to get back on his good side. I didn't want him to be angry with me.

"Uh . . . Mr. Pinker?" I said. "Think I could have another cookie?"

That made him smile.

After the piano lesson, I walked over to Ava's. She lives in a small white house across the street from me. Their garage is almost as big as the house.

My stomach was feeling kind of heavy after eating the two big cookies. And I kept burping up chocolate. I felt a little strange. But I was eager to rehearse my talent show act with Ava and Courtney.

I found them in the kitchen, chopping up vegetables for a salad.

Courtney rolled her big dark eyes and groaned. "Look what the cat dragged in."

"Ha-ha," I said. "Very clever, Courtney. Did you just make that up?"

"How was your piano lesson?" Ava asked. She tossed a big handful of lettuce into the wooden salad bowl on the counter. "Did you sneeze Silly String all over the piano?"

"No way," I said. "I played Chopin."

"And who won?" Courtney asked. "You or Chopin?"

Courtney has a lot of attitude. My mom would say, "She has a sharp mouth."

Actually, I think she's pretty funny. I always know she just teases me because she likes me.

"The show tomorrow is going to be awesome," I said. "You two have to dress alike onstage. Do you know what you're wearing?"

"We already picked out our costumes," Ava said. "We're wearing masks so no one knows who we are."

I pinched her cheek. "I like your enthusiasm!"

My stomach churned. *Two* of those big cookies was definitely one too many.

I turned to Courtney. "Remember about the magic wand? You twirl it above your head like a baton. Then you hand it to Ava, and she sweeps it around and hands it to me."

Courtney sighed. "You mean like we practiced a hundred times?"

"I just want to make sure we're smooth," I said.

I picked up three eggs from a glass bowl, and I started to juggle them in the air.

"Steven, put those down," Ava said. "Mom is making omelets tonight."

"Maybe I'll do a little juggling tomorrow," I said. "I have the three tiny stuffed chickens in my top hat. Maybe I'll pull them out and start juggling them."

I tossed the eggs a little higher. I'm a really good juggler. I have very fast and steady hands. The guy who taught me how to juggle used to be a clown in the Ringling Brothers Circus.

"Steven—please stop," Ava said. "Really."

I tossed the eggs higher. I liked to see the

tense look on her face. Courtney froze by the sink. Her eyes followed the flying eggs.

"Have you ever seen me juggle *five* eggs at once?" I asked.

"Please don't try it," Ava begged.

I tossed the eggs up nearly to the ceiling. My hands were moving so smoothly. Toss. Catch. Toss. Catch.

I had two eggs high in the air when Ava's mom walked into the kitchen.

"NOOOO!" Her scream startled me.

I tossed an egg too high. It *splatted* against the ceiling.

Two eggs came hurtling down. They both landed on Ava's head.

Splat. Splat.

I'll never forget that *cracking* sound.

Ava groaned as gooey yellow egg yolk oozed down her hair, then over her ears and down the sides of her face.

Ava's mom was shaking her head and sighing.

Courtney rushed to Ava and began plucking chunks of broken eggshell from her gooey hair.

I laughed. "Not my bad!" I cried. I pointed at Mrs. Munroe. "She made me do it!"

How come I was the only one in the room laughing?

The gooey stuff ran down Ava's cheeks, down to her neck.

Courtney wrapped her arm around Ava's shoulders and led her from the room. "Don't worry," she told Ava. "We can shampoo it out."

She flashed me a dirty look and led Ava away.

I shouted after them, "Does this mean you don't want to rehearse?"

No answer. Then Courtney called from the hall: "Expect major revenge, Steven."

Revenge? Ha-ha. *Revenge?*

That made me laugh even harder. How could *those two* ever get revenge?

5

I found a surprise waiting at home.

Mom and Dad were huddled in the den. They were clucking and cooing at a creature on the windowsill. They were so intense, they didn't even see me walk in.

I stepped past Dad's big black leather lounger chair into the center of the room. They were fussing over a brown bird.

"Is that a parrot?" I asked.

My parents both spun around. "Oh, hi, Steven," Mom said. "We're not sure. It's the size of a parrot. But it looks more like a baby hawk."

"It flew in the window," Dad said. "It must belong to somebody. It probably flew the coop." He petted the bird's brown feathered head with one finger. "It's very tame."

"Pretty bird," Mom chirped. "Pretty bird. Pretty bird."

I groaned. "Are you two going to talk bird talk from now on?"

"I wasn't talking to the bird. I was talking to *you*," Mom said.

I told you. Everyone in my family is funny.

Mom looks a lot like me. She's short and has round cheeks and dark eyes, and she has straight black hair like mine.

She played jazz piano when she was younger. She says she was a pretty good singer, too. But she gave it up before I was born.

I guess I get a lot of my talent from my family.

Dad is tall and blond, with pale blue eyes. He's kind of rugged looking with broad shoulders and a tough-guy walk.

Mom says he should have been an action-movie star instead of a pediatric surgeon. (Dad operates on children and babies.)

Sometimes he talks about his operations at the dinner table. And Mom and I both cover our ears and scream for him to shut up.

Now they were both sitting on the window seat, cooing at the brown bird perched on the ledge.

"We have to find him a cage," Dad said. "You know — we might have an old one in the basement."

I tossed my backpack on the couch and stepped closer. "You mean we're going to keep him?"

"Your dad has already named him," Mom said. "Bugsy."

"Excuse me?" I said. "Why Bugsy?"

"Because he hunts for bugs and eats them," Dad replied. *"Don't* you, Bugsy? You love bugs, don't you?"

"But he must belong to somebody," I said. "He's not a wild bird—right?"

"We put a lost-and-found notice online," Mom said. "Someone will probably claim him."

"Maybe there's a reward," I said. "Maybe he's worth a million dollars or something."

Dad flashed me his lopsided grin. "Dude! I like the way you think!" He bumped knuckles with me.

I bent down and smoothed my finger down the bird's back. The feathers felt soft and warm.

Bugsy made a sound deep in his throat. It sounded a little like a cat purring.

His little black eyes gleamed. He turned his head, opened his yellow beak, and started to nibble my finger.

"OWWWW!" I jerked my hand back hard. "He BIT me!" I shrieked. "He BIT my FINGER off!"

Mom and Dad both gasped. Their mouths dropped open in horror.

I tossed back my head and laughed. "Gotcha both that time!" I cried. I waved my perfectly okay finger in front of them. "Suckers!"

"You're about as funny as a cold sore," Mom said, shaking her head. "Look. You terrified poor Bugsy. He almost fell off the windowsill."

"There, there, Bugsy," I said. I petted his feathers some more.

He warbled again. Then he turned his beak and licked the tip of my finger.

"Wow! He has a tongue!" I cried. "I didn't know birds had tongues." I laughed. His tongue was dry and scratchy. Like sandpaper.

"Having a pet is very educational," Dad said. "I'll go downstairs and see if I can find that old birdcage."

An idea suddenly flashed into my mind. I gazed at the bird, and a smile spread over my face. "Hey, Bugsy," I said, "I think I have a job for you."

The bird stared up at me as if he was thinking about it.

"Wash your hands before dinner," Mom said.

That night, I locked my bedroom door and practiced my magic act. I always lock the door. If I don't, Mom and Dad come in and give me suggestions.

Sometimes their suggestions are okay. But I really like to plan my own act. Also, a lot of the time, Dad takes my magic wand or my cards or some other stuff and starts doing his own act with them.

I know he does it to be funny. But it's a real pain when I'm trying to rehearse.

Anyway, I practiced until I could barely keep my eyes open. I went through all my usual tricks. And I juggled duckpins for a while. Then I decided not to bring them to the talent assembly. They're too heavy to carry to school.

Later, I had trouble getting to sleep.

Maybe I was too psyched about the show. Or maybe it was my stomach rumbling and grumbling because of Mr. Pinker's big cookies.

I made a promise to myself that at my next piano lesson, I would say no thank you to the cookie. Or maybe eat only *half* of one.

I finally fell asleep after midnight. And I had the stupidest dream.

I dreamed about Bugsy. The brown bird was trapped in a house. For a long time, I couldn't figure out what house it was.

But then I realized it was a little wooden dollhouse.

Was it one of those little dollhouses I saw at Mr. Pinker's house?

In the dream, I bent down and tried to pull him from a little window. But the house started to shrink. And then it was too tiny, maybe an inch or two tall. Too tiny to see Bugsy inside it.

"Bugsy, where are you?" I called in the dream.

Then I woke up and it was morning. Yellow sunlight poured through my open bedroom window. The air smelled fresh and sweet.

The dream quickly faded from my mind. I jumped out of bed and stretched my arms above me. This was talent show day, a day I'd looked forward to for weeks.

I hurried into my clothes. I flew down to breakfast.

I was so excited, I could barely sit still.

How was I to know the day would be a complete disaster?

Some days, the magic just works.

You ever have those times when you know you can't do anything wrong? When everything you do is smooth and easy and wonderful?

That's how the talent assembly started out for me.

The principal gave me a loud, enthusiastic introduction. "Here he is—the Amazing Steven-acious Steven!" The school band played a fanfare. And I came strutting onstage wearing my top hat and twirling the magic wand.

Sure, it's cornball. Sure, it's old-fashioned.

But the kids in the audience ate it up.

And they went wild when Ava and Courtney came following me onstage in their glittery silver tops and shiny leggings.

The act was a total sensation. Even my simplest tricks made the whole auditorium laugh and cheer.

Sometimes my wand sticks and the flower bouquet refuses to pop out. But not today. I swung the wand in front of me — and the flowers appeared. Like magic! Ha-ha.

I took a big sheet of newspaper. I cut it into strips with a scissors. Then I cut the strips into tinier strips. When I unfolded the strips, the paper magically appeared whole again!

Ava and Courtney moved around the stage in time to music by the band. They handed me props and stepped back as I performed the tricks.

Why did they keep grinning at each other?

I thought maybe they were glad the tricks were working and the act was such a hit. I mean, the whole school was watching and loving it.

But their grins were mysterious. I couldn't figure out what they were thinking.

I saw my friend Duncan in the audience. I called him onstage and did a card trick with him. The trick where every card in the deck is the ace of hearts.

Big applause.

Then the two girls paraded around some more. They wheeled in a little table. I got ready to do my *new* trick. I knew the audience would love this one.

My heart started to race. I don't really get nervous onstage. I've never had stage fright. I just love being in front of an audience.

But new tricks always make me a little tense. And I'd practiced this trick for the first time only last night.

The table had a black cloth spread over it. I stepped up to it.

I raised my hands for the band to stop playing. Silence now. I kept my hands raised high over my head.

"Bird of Flight, I summon thee!" I shouted.

Silence.

I glanced out into the auditorium. I had everyone's attention.

Ava and Courtney stood at the sides of the table.

"I summon thee from distant airs!" I shouted. "Bird of Wing, I summon thee to us today!"

Silence.

I lifted the cloth off the table. I raised it high and blocked the table from view.

Then I *snapped* the cloth away—and there stood Bugsy.

I lowered my hand, and the brown bird jumped onto my arm. I raised the bird high as kids cheered and clapped.

I turned and caught Ava and Courtney smiling. Of course, they'd never seen my Bugsy trick. I could tell they liked it.

I held Bugsy high so everyone could see him. The bird lowered his head and licked my cheek. More than once. I guess he was giving me a kiss.

I felt a chill. His tongue felt so dry and scratchy against my skin.

I handed him to Ava and told her to put Bugsy in the cage backstage.

Now it was time for my big finish.

Courtney handed me four red rubber balls, my juggling balls. This was the hardest stunt I'd ever tried.

I planned to juggle the four balls, keeping two in the air the whole time. And to drink a cup of water while I juggled them.

The three of us had practiced this day after day. Some days, it worked very well. Sometimes, I dropped the balls when I started to drink. A few times, I choked on the water.

But today everything was working. Everything was perfect.

I never felt so much in control. So much confidence.

The Steven-acious Steven was a winner!

The band played a fanfare. I stepped to the edge of the stage and started to juggle. Three red balls at first, slowly. Then, as I picked up speed, I added the fourth ball.

Two up. Two down. Two up. Two down.

I had the balls going in a perfect rhythm. I felt like a machine, a juggling machine.

A drumroll by the snare drummer.

Courtney stepped forward. She carried the

paper cup in front of her. The cup was filled half-way up with water.

I shouted to the audience: "In a trick that only the Steven-acious Steven performs, I will now juggle and drink a cup of water at the same time!"

I could see everyone's eyes on me. No one moved or talked.

Two up. Two down. Two up. Two down.

I kept the rhythm going. The red balls made a *snapping* sound as they slapped into my moving hands.

Courtney stepped closer. She raised the blue paper cup to my lips.

Two up. Two down. Two up. Two down.

Courtney tilted the cup to my mouth.

I took a long sip.

A bitter liquid burned my tongue. A horrible sick taste filled my mouth.

"*AAAAAAAGH!*" A hoarse scream burst from my throat.

I batted the cup away. Courtney leaped back.

The four red balls bounced all around me. They thudded on the stage floor and bounced into the audience.

The sharp sour taste in my mouth made me sick. My stomach *heaved.*

"I've been POISONED!" I screamed. "Somebody—help! I've been POISONED!"

The sour taste puckered my lips. I started to gag.

I knew I was going to hurl. With another cry, I turned and ran off the stage.

I could hear the roar of laughter in the auditorium. Kids were shrieking and laughing their heads off.

It was a riot back there. I could hear teachers shouting for everyone to get quiet. A few teachers came running to help me.

I cupped my hand over my mouth and ran to the bathroom backstage. But by the time I got there, my stomach had settled down a little. I didn't feel like puking anymore.

I leaned against the wall, trying to settle myself. Trying to think clearly about what had just happened.

My act was going beautifully, perfectly—and then it was *ruined*.

But how? Why?

Then I saw Ava and Courtney come staggering toward me. They were hugging each other, slapping high fives, laughing.

Why were they *celebrating*?

"Wh-what happened?" I stammered. I still felt queasy. The burning sour taste lingered in my mouth. I kept swallowing. Swallowing. Trying to get rid of it.

"What happened? What was in that paper cup? What did you give me?"

I lurched to the water fountain on the wall and gulped down about a gallon. Then I turned back to them. They were still giggling and enjoying themselves.

I grabbed each one by the arm. "Tell me. What did you put in that cup?"

They finally stopped giggling.

"Just something we mixed up in the chem lab," Courtney said.

"Huh? Are you *serious*?" I shrieked.

They both nodded.

"You gave me *chemicals* to drink?" I cried.

They laughed.

"We just poured in whatever we could find," Ava said. "You know. We pulled bottles off the shelf and poured them in."

I grabbed my throat. "But—but—why?" I sputtered.

"You deserved it," they both said at the same time. Then they spun away and took off, running to the backstage door.

"I — I've been . . . poisoned," I murmured. I stood there, my heart pounding, my brain spinning.

I could still taste the bitter chemicals on my tongue. My stomach lurched again.

I forced myself to move. I picked up Bugsy in his metal birdcage. And I ran out the back door.

Into the sunny, cool afternoon. I ran across the empty playground. I flew across the street without checking for traffic.

I ran without seeing, without thinking. Ran all the way home.

I burst through the kitchen door. Set Bugsy's cage down on the counter.

And started to shout: "Mom! Dad! Help me!"

No one home.

I swallowed some more. I tried to fight down my panic.

I'm okay. I'm okay, I told myself.

I'll brush my teeth, I decided. *That will get rid of this putrid taste.*

I ran to the stairs — and stumbled into a bucket and mop. Water sloshed over my sneakers and made a soapy puddle on the floor.

Mom or Dad must have been mopping the floor and left the mop and pail at the bottom of the stairs.

I stepped around it and pulled myself up the stairs two at a time.

The upstairs hall felt warmer than downstairs. It smelled piney up here. Someone had definitely been cleaning. Probably Dad. He's the big cleaner in our family.

I passed the guest room, then my room. The bathroom was at the end of the hall.

"Hey!" I let out a startled shout. And stumbled into the wall.

I pushed both hands against the pale pink wallpaper and spun around.

What just happened? It took me a few seconds to realize. I was standing barefoot on the dark purple carpet.

I'd stepped right out of my sneakers.

But — how? They were tightly laced.

I left them in the middle of the floor and walked down the hall.

Nearly to the bathroom, I tripped over my jeans.

Huh? Why are my pants falling off?

I hitched them up with one hand. I felt strange, a little dizzy. I blinked a few times. The wallpaper seemed to be rising up on both sides of me.

I glanced up. That made me feel even dizzier. The ceiling suddenly appeared much higher than usual. The bathroom door rose a mile over my head.

Was something wrong with my eyes?

My tongue felt dry. Kind of itchy. I could taste the sour chemicals on the roof of my mouth.

It's going to take a lot of toothpaste to get rid of this taste, I thought.

I stepped up to the sink and reached for my toothbrush.

"Whoooaaa!"

What's up with this?

Why did I have to stand on tiptoe to reach over the sink?

My arms weren't long enough to reach the toothbrush in its cup. I had to jump high to grab it.

I wrapped my hand around it. The toothbrush felt so heavy. I had to hold it in both hands.

Whoa. Wait. Wait . . .

My head barely poked above the sink. I couldn't reach the faucet.

I didn't want to believe it. But I had no choice.

I stood there, my whole body trembling. My teeth began to chatter in fear. The toothbrush was almost as big as a baseball bat!

"I . . . can't be shrinking," I murmured. My voice came out so tiny and high.

"I can't be shrinking. That's impossible— right?"

That's when the clothes fell off my body. My jeans fell to the floor and sagged around me. My T-shirt slid off and puddled around my ankles.

I stood there totally naked and stared up at the sink high above my head.

"It's impossible—right? I can't be shrinking."

10

I stepped away from the pile of my clothes. My socks were as big as our laundry bags.

I hugged myself to try to keep from trembling. I stood there, naked, staring up at the bottom of the sink high above me.

I felt totally strange. My heart was beat-beat-beating like I had a hummingbird inside me. A water drip in the sink made me jump. The loud noise rang like a bell clanging.

I hugged myself tighter. I was numb with fright. I mean, my skin felt cold and numb. I couldn't stop my teeth from chattering.

How short am I? I wondered.

I turned. I was standing beside the bathroom scale. It was too tall to step up on. I had to hoist myself up using both hands.

How much did I weigh? I stood on the scale. But I was too light to make it go down. The dial showed *zero*.

That sent a shudder down my already cold back.

I hopped down from the scale. I couldn't tell how tall I was. Maybe six inches tall, maybe eight or nine.

Did it matter?

I thought Ava and Courtney were my friends. But they gave me chemicals that made me shrink. They *poisoned* me!

Okay, okay. I took a deep breath and held it. But it didn't help me fight back my panic.

Okay. They wanted revenge. But how could they do this to me? *How?*

Then a question flashed into my panicked mind. A question that sent shivers of fear down my tiny body.

Was I going to be a tiny person for the rest of my life?

11

No. Impossible.

I had to get back to my normal size. I had to sit down and *think*.

I had to get to my room. I had to figure out something. Make a plan. *Do* something!

And I had to find something to wear.

I ran out of the bathroom. My feet slapped the floor tiles but barely made a sound.

Out into the hall. The purple carpet was thick and tall. It came up over my ankles and scratched my legs.

I saw my sneakers halfway down the hall. They looked like big boats riding on a purple lake.

What can I wear?

I couldn't walk around naked.

I stepped into my room. The bed rose up like a mountain. I had to crane my neck to see to the top of my bookshelves.

I'd left a pile of dirty clothes on the floor. But

of course they were all too big. I tried to pull up a white sock. It was almost as tall as me. And too heavy to wrap around me.

I sat down on a bunched-up pair of jeans to think. What could I wear? What would fit me?

I realized that maybe I was staring at the answer. On the bottom bookshelf. My two marionettes.

One was a clown in a red-and-white polka-dot clown costume. That wouldn't be very good. But the other marionette was a man in a brown business suit.

Of course, I'd look totally lame in a brown business suit made for a puppet. But I was only six or eight inches tall. I really couldn't be choosy.

I ran to the bookshelf. I kept tripping on the white shag rug.

I lowered my shoulder and pushed through the thicket of wool. It was like fighting my way through a jungle. The wool stuck to my legs and scratched my knees. It seemed to take an *hour* to reach the shelf.

I fumbled with the two marionettes. They were bigger than I'd thought. It took all my strength to push the clown marionette away.

I reached for the businessman. The puppet was on its back, staring up. The strings were tangled all around it.

I struggled to push the strings away so I could sit the puppet up. Undressing it wasn't going to be easy.

I tugged off the shiny black shoes. They were made of some kind of plastic. Would they fit me?

Only one way to find out.

I dropped onto the edge of the bookshelf. Gripped the left shoe in both hands — and pulled it on.

Yes! It was my size!

I didn't celebrate. What a horrifying thought. My foot was the same size as a puppet foot!

I pulled on the other shoe and stood up. I tried walking along the edge of the shelf. The plastic shoes squeaked. They were a little tight. But at least they covered my bare feet.

I tried to stand the puppet up, but I wasn't strong enough. It was taller than me. I had to try to pull the suit off with the marionette lying on its back.

I dropped to my hands and knees and started to pull off the marionette's silky suit pants. I grabbed the waist and tried to tug down. But the pants didn't move.

I pulled harder.

Then I saw that I was wasting my time. The puppet's strings were nailed to its body. And the nails went through the clothes.

No way could I tug the pants off without

ripping them to pieces. Or getting them completely tangled in the strings.

With a sigh, I jumped down off the bookshelf.

There I was, less than ten inches tall, totally naked except for squeaky black plastic shoes. Frantically, I gazed around my room.

What could I wear?

I blinked when I saw the two dolls on the floor at the foot of the bed. It took me a few seconds to remember that my little cousin Mindy had left them there the last time she visited.

I stumbled back through the tall wool of the shag rug. Finally, I stopped and stared at the two dolls. Barbie and Ken.

Barbie was in her doctor outfit—white lab coat and a surgeon's cap. Her hair was tied back. She had a stethoscope around her neck. And she wore glasses.

Ken wore flashy rock-and-roll clothes. A sparkly silver jumpsuit with a neon blue shirt underneath, open to the waist. Lots of fake gold chains around his neck.

I knew this outfit wasn't nailed to his body. Because Mindy was constantly changing their outfits. Would Ken's clothes fit me?

Yes. Actually, the shirt was a little loose. The jumpsuit pants were too long, so I rolled up the bottoms. The gold chains I tossed aside.

Okay, I looked like a total freak. But at least I was dressed.

Now I had to calm down. Concentrate. Get my brain chugging.

Ava and Courtney gave me chemicals to drink. And the chemicals made me shrink.

I had to reach them. I had to find out exactly what they put in that paper cup.

If I knew what I drank, maybe ... just maybe ... our doctor or *someone* would know what I could drink to make me tall again.

Okay. I decided to call Ava first.

Gazing up, I saw my cell phone on the bed.

The bed rose over me like Mount Everest. The phone seemed miles away.

I had to reach it. I had to get up there. But *how*?

12

I grabbed the wooden leg of the bed with both hands. I jumped off the floor and wrapped my legs around it.

I was never a good climber. I could never get to the top of the rope in gym class. And I hated the wall-climbing place at the mall.

But I had to be a good climber now.

Luckily, the little plastic shoes helped. They stuck to the wooden leg and held tight as I worked my way slowly up.

My hands were sweaty. I'd climb a few inches. Plant my feet. Reach up another few inches. But my damp hands kept sliding back down.

Halfway up, I made the mistake of looking down to the floor.

"Whoooaa!"

I've always had a problem with heights.

Now I felt dizzy. The room was spinning. I gripped the leg tightly and returned my gaze to the top of the bed.

Still a long way to go.

I raised my hands. Clamped them around the leg. Pushed up with the plastic shoes.

To my shock, the shoes slipped. My wet hands started to slide.

I lost my hold and started to drop.

"Noooo!" a shrill scream escaped my throat as I fell straight down.

I made a desperate grab. Swung both hands out.

And gripped the side of the bedspread.

"Yesssss!"

My hands tightened around the heavy red-and-white fabric. My body slammed into the side of the bed. But I held on tight.

I dug the shoes into the bedspread. Raised my hands and started to climb again.

By the time I reached the top of the bed, my whole body was shaking. Sweat poured down my face.

I lay facedown on the bedspread for a minute or two, struggling to catch my breath. I waited for my arms and legs to stop aching from the climb.

Pushing myself up to my knees, I let out a sad sigh. I suddenly pictured myself jumping out of bed in the morning. Or, sitting on the side of the bed, my feet resting on the floor.

Would I ever be able to do those things again? Would getting into bed at night always be like climbing a tall mountain? Would Mom and Dad have to buy me some kind of baby bed or maybe a dog bed to sleep in?

Crazy thoughts. But do you blame me?

I shook myself, trying to force those thoughts away. And I crawled over to the phone.

Up close, it appeared bigger than a suitcase. It's a flip phone. So the first thing I had to do was flip it open.

I gripped the lid with both hands and pushed. To my surprise, it swung up easily. *Yaaay!*

The screen lit up with my screen saver—a magician's top hat with a rabbit poking out of it.

I sighed again. My magic act at school killed. It was awesome. But then Ava and Courtney pulled the best trick of all—making me smaller than a rabbit.

"You'll be back, Steven," I said out loud. "This can be fixed. You'll be back, dude."

I was trying to cheer myself up. But it didn't work.

I had to call Ava. I had to know what chemicals she and Courtney put in that cup.

I bent over the phone and lowered my hands to the keyboard. The keys were gigantic—as big as my mom's pancakes.

I leaned forward and started to push Ava's number.

"Unnnh." I groaned as I tried to push the speed-dial button down. It didn't budge.

I leaned closer and spread both hands over it. Then I shoved my hands down with all my strength.

No.

Not happening.

My little hands weren't strong enough to push the key down.

Now what?

Now what?

I pounded both fists on the button. Pounded furiously. But it wouldn't click.

I could feel my panic start to choke my throat. I froze staring down at the giant phone keys.

Suddenly, I had an idea.

13

I climbed to my feet and stepped onto the phone.

My plastic shoes squeaked as I walked onto the keyboard. I stood on Ava's speed-dial key. Leaped up—and stomped down on it with all my strength.

Beep. The number clicked.

Then, breathing hard, I jumped on the SEND key.

A few seconds later, I could hear the ring. It was so loud, I nearly fell off the phone.

It rang once . . . twice . . .

I heard a *click*. And then Ava's voice. A roar in my tiny ears.

"Steven? Hello?"

"Ava—you've got to help me!" I cried.

A pause. Then Ava's booming voice again: "Hello? Steven? Is that you?"

"Ava—listen to me!" My voice came out

squeaky like a mouse. I tried to shout louder. "I need help! I need you to help me!"

"Steven—I can't hear you," Ava said. "Are you there? I know it's you, Steven. Your name came up. Is this a joke?"

"No, Ava—please—" I begged. "Listen harder. It's not a joke. It's me."

"It's a bad connection," she said. "I can't hear a thing. Call me back."

"NO!" I screamed. "I can't call you back! It's too hard. I need your help!"

"Steven? Are you there? *Say* something!" she shouted. "You're not funny."

And then, a deafening *click*. Like a clap of thunder.

Ava hung up on me.

I dropped to my knees on top of the phone. My head still rang from Ava's loud voice.

Now what? Wait for Mom and Dad to help me?

I suddenly remembered they were going to be out late tonight. I was supposed to walk to my cousin Mindy's house and have dinner there.

Mindy could help me. But wait. Her house was at least eight or nine blocks away. At my new size, that could take me *days*!

Ava lived across the street. A much shorter walk.

Could I make it to Ava's house? I had no choice. I had to risk it.

My first problem — getting down from the bed. I gazed at the floor again. A mistake. A wave of dizziness made me sit down.

Too far to jump. Even with the shag rug beneath me, I could break every bone in my body.

I sat on the edge of the bed and turned to the bedpost. Could I slide down it like a fire pole?

I might slide too fast and burn all the skin off my little hands.

Could I lower myself slowly and carefully down the bedpost?

That's what I was thinking when the phone rang.

The sound made me jump. I uttered a startled scream. *"AAAAAIIIIH!"*

And fell off the bed.

14

I fell feetfirst. My back slid down the side of the bedspread.

WHUMMP.

I landed on my knees and fell face forward into the shag rug.

My breath rushed out in a whoosh. I bounced once, then rolled onto my back, choking and wheezing.

A few seconds later, I pulled myself to my feet. I moved my arms up and down and bent my knees. Testing everything out. No broken bones.

The shag rug saved my life. Now I had pieces of white lint all over the front of my silvery jumpsuit. But I didn't care. I was in one piece, ready for the next part of my journey.

A difficult task—climbing down the stairs.

I walked past my old sneakers in the middle of the hall. I wished I could wear them. My new plastic puppet shoes were too tight and really pinched my toes.

I stopped at the top of the stairs and looked down. The stairs were steep and stretched straight down, like a deep cavern. At the bottom, I could see the mop and water pail I had tripped over before.

No way I could step down the normal way. My feet just wouldn't reach.

I realized I had to turn around and lower myself down one step at a time.

"No problem," I said out loud. "It's just like climbing down a ladder."

I was trying to psych myself up again.

Steven, you perform all kinds of magic tricks. Pretend this is a new trick you are doing. Pretend you have an audience watching you, and you want to impress them.

Sure, I could tell myself all kinds of stuff. I could pretend this was as easy as doing a card trick or juggling little red balls.

But when I did magic tricks, I wasn't exactly *risking my life.*

I turned my back to the front of the stairs. I lowered myself to my knees. Then I gripped the edge of the top step and slowly . . . carefully . . . lowered myself.

I wasn't tall enough. My feet wouldn't touch the next step. I had to let go of the step above me and *drop* onto the lower step.

"*Ow.*" I landed hard on my plastic shoes and struggled to gain my balance.

One stair down. Many more to go.

I gripped the edge of the stair above me. The wood was slippery. Mom or Dad must have mopped and polished the stairs.

I tightened my hands on it and carefully lowered myself to the next step.

My heart was pounding. But I felt a little better. It was hard on my arm muscles. But this wasn't as tough as I thought it would be.

I could do this.

I glanced down at the water bucket again. I moved far to the left. I wanted to make sure I didn't come anywhere near that bucket.

I took a deep breath and gripped the step above me.

I lowered myself carefully, then dropped onto another step. And then another.

A piece of cake. My arms ached. But I was halfway down the stairs.

I lowered myself one more step.

And then opened my mouth in a scream of horror as something grabbed me by the legs.

A giant mouse!

15

"Let GO!" I screamed.

The creature was *swallowing* me whole!

No. Wait.

I thrashed my arms and kicked at it.

Wait. Not a mouse.

A dust ball. A huge dust ball nearly as tall as me.

Mom and Dad must not have mopped this far.

The thick gray dust clung to my skin, my clothes. I'd dropped right into the middle of it. Now it was holding me prisoner.

I brushed the sticky dry stuff away from my face. Pulled it off the front of my jump-suit. Kicking and swinging my arms, I pushed out of it.

It clung to my back. I swung around and slapped at it. I couldn't get free.

I swung my body around again, trying to slip away from it—

—and fell off the step!

I opened my mouth to scream, but no sound came out.

I tumbled onto the next step. My head hit the hard wood with a loud *thud*.

I shut my eyes as pain bolted through my body. I somersaulted off the step. Hit the next one. Bounced hard.

Smacked my head again on the next step. I let out a groan as my whole body throbbed with pain.

I shoved out both hands, struggling to stop my fall. But I was hurtling too fast now.

I rolled over the edge of another step—

—and SPLASH.

Cold water washed over me as I sank into the soapy water pail.

I shot my arms up above my head. But I couldn't stop myself from sinking to the bottom.

The water felt greasy and the soap made it impossible for me to see. It burned my eyes. And held me down as I struggled to swim to the surface.

It was like trying to swim in thick pea soup. Finally, I pulled myself to the top of the thick, mucky water. Choking and sputtering, I sucked in a deep breath.

The piney detergent smell choked my throat. My nose burned. My eyes watered. I kicked and slapped the water, struggling to keep afloat.

But how long could I swim in this stuff?

I gazed up to the top of the bucket. Too high for me to reach. I pulled myself to the side and tried to scramble up. But I slid right back into the water.

No way to climb out. And I wasn't strong enough to tip the bucket over onto its side so I could be washed out.

I swam in frantic circles, around and around. My mind whirred. How to get out . . . How to get out . . .

My chest started to burn. My arms were getting heavy. I tried floating on my back for a while. But I couldn't float and swim in here forever.

Mom and Dad weren't getting home till late. No way I could last till they arrived.

I turned over and started to swim again, doing a slow, lazy breaststroke. The soap burned my eyes and nose. The sharp odor made it hard to breathe.

My arms ached and throbbed. I knew I couldn't keep swimming much longer.

I couldn't help it. I let out a sob.

Was I really going to drown in a bucket of soapy water?

My chest hurt. Pain shot down my chest . . . my arms . . . my legs . . .

Can't keep swimming. Can't do it.
Can't breathe . . . Can't swim anymore . . .

I gave up. My whole body slumped. I folded up like a paper bag—and sank into the cold, greasy water.

16

As I started to go down, a shadow rolled over me.

I turned my face to the surface. What made that sound? Like a flap of wind.

Using my last bit of strength, I pulled myself toward the top. My head bobbed up from the water. Blinking away the burning suds, I stared up into the shadow. A shadow that flapped and shimmered above me.

Bugsy!

The flutter of his wings sent the water churning. The waves tossed me from one side of the bucket to the other.

The bird appeared *enormous* now. Like an airplane rocketing down at me. The dark eyes were as big as basketballs. And the bird's yellow beak . . . clicked open and shut . . . open and shut . . . like hedge clippers.

The beak snapped at me, splashing the surface of the tossing water.

"No!" I cried out, and ducked my head.

Sputtering in the soapy water, I raised my arms to shield myself.

Bugsy attacked again. The giant beak snapped at my head. Water splashed hard. I felt myself tossed against the side of the metal bucket.

"Bugsy — no!"

He flapped above the bucket, then swooped again.

And then the giant beak clamped around my waist. I felt it cut into my skin.

The bird flapped his wings rapidly. I let out a cry as he lifted me from the water. And carried me high into the air.

"Bugsy — let me down!" My voice came out in a tiny squeak.

I thrashed my arms and legs. Carrying me like a robin carries a worm, the bird swooped across the living room.

"Let me down! Let me down!" The sharp beak cut into my sides.

And then the bird opened his jaws, and I tumbled out.

I hit the living room floor, landing on my stomach. *"Oof!"* My breath whooshed out of my lungs. Gasping for air, I shot my arms out and tried to crawl to safety.

On the windowsill I saw the new cage my parents had bought for Bugsy. The door was wide open. Bugsy had busted out.

Now the big bird swooped down and snapped me in his beak again. He lifted me high off the floor. And dropped me. Then lifted me. And dropped me again.

I landed hard on my side. My ribs throbbed in pain.

I rolled onto my back. Raised both hands to shield myself. But I was helpless against the huge bird.

"Bugsy, please. No! No!"

I waved my hands furiously. The bird ducked his head under them—and lifted me off the floor again.

Dropped me. Lifted me. Dropped me.

I felt too weak to fight him. My body went limp from the pain.

He thinks I'm a bug, I realized.

He's playing with me—before he EATS me!

17

Thud.

I hit the floor again. I felt weak. My arms and legs still ached from swimming around in the bucket. My whole body hurt from hitting the floor again and again.

The bird lowered his beak to grab me again.

With a groan, I rolled away from him. The diving beak missed me and bumped the floor. The bird uttered a squawk, surprised.

Panting hard, I scrambled away. Half crawling, half rolling across the floor.

The shadow of the bird's wings swept over the floor as he turned and came after me. He came darting down fast.

I dove for cover—under the couch.

Wheezing loudly, my chest pounding in pain, I pressed myself low. I peered out from under the couch.

I could see Bugsy land. His enormous feet clawed at the floor. He made a warbling sound from deep in his throat.

Still struggling to catch my breath, I watched the bird pace back and forth in front of the couch. Just inches from my face.

He was searching everywhere for me. But he didn't look under the couch.

Birdbrain. The word flashed in my mind. How lucky was I that birds aren't very smart?

Lucky probably wasn't the right word. This wasn't exactly my lucky day.

The bird had vanished from my sight. Maybe he flew back to his perch. Or maybe he was waiting off to the side, waiting for me to leave my hiding place.

I heard a scrabbling sound behind me. A fast tap-tap-tapping.

My stomach pressed against the floor. I twisted my head around and squinted into the darkness under the couch.

"Oh, no!" A cry escaped my throat as an enormous creature scuffled toward me.

It took me a few seconds to realize it was a spider. A spider out of a *horror movie*!

The space beneath the couch was filled with thick cobwebs. The huge spider came tearing through the tangle of webs.

Shiny and black, with blazing red eyes the size of Ping-Pong balls. Its legs were as thick as drinking straws.

I'd never seen spiders' teeth before. But I saw them now, gnashing up and down. Thick white drool poured over the pointed teeth from the open mouth.

The gleaming red eyes stared hungrily straight ahead. *Tap-tap-tap*. It picked up speed, eager to reach its prey. *Me!*

With a gasp, I raised myself and started to crawl out from under the couch.

But I stopped. Was Bugsy waiting for me just out of view? Waiting to devour me, the bug he had tortured?

My mind spun. I had to make a choice. A horrifying choice: Stay under the couch and fight the spider? Or crawl out and face Bugsy?

My hand bumped something on the floor. I gripped it and pulled it closer.

It took me a moment to recognize it — a toothpick. A wooden toothpick. It looked longer than a *sword* to me.

Could I use it as a weapon against the spider?

I grabbed it off the dusty floor. I tried to raise it. I wasn't strong enough to lift it with one hand. I had to use two.

Tap-tap-tap. The spider legs clicked across the floor as the fat creature marched toward me.

I struggled to hold the toothpick sword steady in front of me. It quivered in my hands.

Could I bat the big insect away with it? Could I stab the spider? Pin it with the toothpick?

Tap-tap-tap. It came clicking closer, gnashing its jaws, drooling.

I lowered the toothpick point toward its belly.

But the spider seemed to have no fear of the weapon. It just kept on bouncing and clicking forward.

Closer . . . closer . . .

I held my breath. I tightened my grip. Made a sharp stabbing move with the toothpick.

The spider grabbed the end of the toothpick with two thick legs. It began to climb onto it!

"Nooooo!" a terrified cry escaped my throat.

I let the toothpick fall to the floor.

Then I rolled away. Spun my body out from under the couch.

Blinking in the sudden bright light, I scrambled to my knees. Heart pounding, I looked behind me.

The spider moved quickly across the floor. It clicked and tapped its way out from under the couch. It moved in a straight line. The big body bobbed from side to side, but the eyes stayed on me. It wasn't going to give up its prey so easily.

I struggled to my feet. Tried to run.

Then I heard the flapping above me. And saw Bugsy floating overhead.

I was trapped. Caught out in the open. Nowhere to hide. No way to fight them.

The spider was inches behind me. Above me, the giant bird spread his wings. Lowered his head. And dove.

18

"AAAIIIII!"

I let out a scream as the spider shot out two legs and grabbed me by the shoulders. The hard, stiff legs dug into my skin.

With incredible strength, it pulled me toward its gaping mouth. I struggled to free myself. But I was no match for it.

I opened my mouth to scream again—but stopped as the shadow of the bird covered me in darkness.

I heard a sharp *snap*. Saw the huge beak swoop down in front of me—and grab the spider!

"Huh?" I uttered a startled gasp as Bugsy tightened his beak over the spider. The bird lifted the spider off the floor. Turned and flapped away with it.

For a few seconds, I didn't move. I stood there shaking. I could still feel the hard pinch of the spider's legs on my shoulders. And I couldn't get that gaping, drool-covered mouth from my mind.

I took a deep breath and held it. I knew I had to get out of the house—fast. Bugsy wouldn't be happy with his spider meal. He'd be back looking for me—the other bug—any second.

I knew what I had to do. I had to get to Ava's house. I had to find out what she and Courtney gave me to drink.

But could I get all the way across the street to Ava's house?

My trip down the stairs had been a nightmare. Would I have to fight every ant, every squirrel, every bunny rabbit, every bug hiding in our front yards to get there?

I had no choice. I had to try.

My heart still thudding in my chest, I ran to the front door. I stopped a few feet in front of it, gazing up at the doorknob high above my head.

Problem Number One: How to open the door?

I gazed down at the crack under the door. Too narrow for me to squeeze through.

I studied the doorknob. Even if I could reach it, I wouldn't be strong enough to turn it.

And the door was probably locked. That meant turning the knob above the doorknob.

No way. No way. No way.

I heard Bugsy chirp somewhere behind me. The sound sent a chill racing down my back.

I knew I didn't have much time. But what could I do?

"Hey — wait!" I slapped my forehead. I stared at the mail slot. I was tiny enough to slip through it.

Then I saw the pair of boots standing at the door. My dad's boots, the tall ones he wears to go hunting in the deep woods.

I grabbed the toe of the nearest boot and rubbed my hands over the rough leather. Then I raised my eyes to the thick crisscross of laces.

I knew what I had to do. Hoist myself onto the toe of the boot. Then use the laces as a rope ladder. Climb the laces. Pull myself to the top of the boot.

That would take me almost to the mail slot.

If I could lift the metal lid of the mail slot, I could slide through it. And drop onto the front stoop.

Another bird chirp in the room behind me moved me to action.

I pressed both hands flat on the toe of the boot — and heaved myself onto it. I stayed on my hands and knees, waiting to catch my balance.

Then I crawled over the toe to the bottom of the laces. The laces felt rough in my hands. They were as thick as ropes.

I wrapped both hands around the bottom laces and pulled myself to a standing position. Then I grabbed the next crisscross of laces.

I gazed up. This wasn't going to be easy. It was like climbing a mountain that rose *straight up.*

I pulled myself higher. And dug my plastic shoes into the laces beneath me.

I found I could lean my weight against the tongue of the boot as I carefully pulled myself up.

One more row of laces. Then the next.

My arms ached. The scratchy laces had turned my hands red. Leaning on the tongue, I dug my shoes into the X of laces beneath me. And tugged myself up higher.

I was breathing hard. Sweat poured down my face as I reached the top of the boot.

I gripped the worn leather at the top. The mail slot shimmered just a few inches over my head.

I can do this! I told myself. *I can do this!* I let go of the boot—and flung myself at the mail slot lid.

But my shoes caught on the edge of the boot.

My hands grabbed *air.*

And I started to fall. Headfirst. Inside the boot.

Into the cavelike darkness of the boot.

Down . . . down . . . Screaming all the way.

19

"OWWW!"

I landed hard on one shoulder. My body thudded onto the leather bottom of the boot.

I rolled onto my back and tried to shake off the pain. It was dark down here and smelly. I grabbed the wall of the boot. The leather was smooth. I slid right back down.

I raised my eyes to the top. Pale light poured down from the opening above me.

I pressed both hands against the side and tried to climb. Too slippery and nothing to hold on to. No way I could get back to the top. And I was too small to push the tongue away and climb back to the laces.

I was stuck.

I tried to hold my breath. The smell down here was sharp and gross. It smelled like sweat and damp socks.

I'd been so close . . . so close to grabbing the mail slot.

Angrily, I slammed my fist against the wall of the boot.

That gave me an idea. I shoved both fists into the side of the boot. I felt it tilt a little.

I lowered my shoulder and slammed it into the boot wall. Then I dove to the other side and shoved against it.

The boot was rocking from side to side. I pushed one side, then dove into the other side. I whirled from side to side, making the boot tilt harder . . .

. . . until it toppled over.

"Whooooaaa!"

I went sliding out headfirst. It was like going down a long waterslide—without the water.

The boot rocked onto its side, and I came tumbling out.

I didn't wait to catch my breath. One boot lay on its side. The other boot stood straight up in front of the door.

I scrambled to the other boot. I hoisted myself onto the toe, crawled to the laces—and began the long, steep climb again.

A little while later, I gripped the top of the boot. The metal mail slot stood inches in front of me.

Slowly, I edged myself over the side of the boot. I reached one hand out and grabbed the lid of the mail slot.

This time I wasn't going to leap at the slot.

This time I wanted to be careful. This could be my last chance to escape Bugsy and get out of the house.

Could I lift the mail slot lid with one hand? I leaned forward and gave it a tug.

No. Too heavy for my little hands.

I leaned farther out of the boot and gripped the lid of the mail slot with both hands.

"Ohhhh!"

I felt the boot start to fall from under me.

I gripped the mail slot and held on for dear life as the boot fell onto its side.

My feet dangled in the air. Instantly, my arms started to ache. My hands throbbed as I hung on tightly to the lid.

With a burst of strength, I swung my body up—and YES! YES!

My feet shot out through the slot. I let go of the lid and sailed right through.

"Ooof!" I landed hard on my butt on the welcome mat. I waited for the pain to fade. Then I stretched my arms and legs to make sure nothing was broken.

I gazed across my front yard. I saw only shades of gray and black. It took me a few moments to realize the sun had dropped behind the trees. It wasn't afternoon anymore. It was evening.

"Hey!" I raised my arm to shield myself as two flies buzzed around my head. The flies were as big as bats!

I could see Ava's house across the street. I could usually run there in less than a minute. But now, her house seemed a mile or two away. And the sloping front lawn looked like a mountain.

A funny thought flashed into my mind. Maybe my cousin Mindy's rock-and-roll Ken doll came with a little motorcycle. I could ride it across the street to Ava's house.

Of course, it was a stupid idea. There was no way I'd risk going back into my house to find out.

But riding would definitely be better than walking.

I turned and lowered myself off the stoop, one step at a time, the way I'd climbed down the stairs.

The shortest way was right down the center of the lawn. But the grass was tall—up to my waist. I moved into it, brushing the high blades away with my shoulder.

The grass bent easily. But the sharp edges of the blades scratched my face and hands as I pushed my way toward the sidewalk.

It was slow going. The air grew cooler. The sky darkened to purple.

I was about a third of the way down the front lawn when my foot caught on something. I stumbled. Lurched forward. Both feet kicked only air.

And I fell into a deep darkness. A pit. Hidden by the grass.

A deep hole.

"Hey!" I landed on both feet. My hands shot out and touched a cool, damp wall of dirt.

I glanced up. The hole was deep. But I could probably climb the dirt wall.

Something poked my back.

I let out a startled cry. I spun around. Too dark to see.

Something poked my chest.

I reached out both hands. And felt something sticky and wet.

Something warm.

And alive.

20

I jerked my hands back. Squinting hard, I struggled to see what was sharing the hole with me.

It rubbed my face. It was wet and slimy. My skin prickled.

I felt it wrap itself around my neck. It smelled strong, like dirt. And its skin was wet and wrinkly and gluey.

It slid away, leaving my skin wet. It raised itself in front of me.

And in the dim evening light, I saw what it was — a worm.

Just a common earthworm. Not too frightening — unless you are six inches tall!

To me, it was as big as a python.

It curled around my waist. I grabbed its slimy, wet middle. I struggled to pry it off. But I couldn't budge it.

I shot both hands out and felt something above my head. Looking up, I realized it was a root. Some kind of underground tree root.

I gripped it with both hands.

I swung myself up onto the root. Then I squirmed and thrashed and kicked till the worm finally loosened its grip.

I tugged myself up the root. Grabbed the dirt wall with both hands. And scrambled up the side of the hole.

Gasping for breath, I dove into the grass. I lay there panting for a long time. I kept glancing back to see if the giant worm would follow me. But it stayed down in the hole.

I stood up on shaky legs. My glittery Ken jumpsuit was soaking wet from worm slime. I tried to brush dirt off the front. But it clung to the sticky fabric.

I knew I would totally gross out Ava. But I didn't care. It was all Ava's fault that I was in this frightening mess.

A short while later, I stepped out of the grass and onto the sidewalk. Across the street, the lights were on in Ava's house.

A car rolled past. The headlights blinded me. I shut my eyes and waited for the circles of light to fade.

I opened my eyes. The street was dark again. Could I make it across the street before another car came by?

I took a deep breath. I tensed my whole body. I knew I had to run faster than I'd ever run in my life. If a car came down the block, there was no way the driver would see me.

I looked up and down the street again. Silent and dark.

Here goes.

My plastic shoes scraped the pavement as I began to run across the street. It wasn't a big street, but it looked as long as a football field to me!

I leaped over pebbles. I swung my arms and leaned forward as I ran.

I was halfway across, running hard, when I heard voices.

I stopped in the middle of the street. Turned — and saw two gigantic kids on gigantic bikes pedaling furiously right at me.

21

I cried out. But, of course, they couldn't hear me.

I tried waving my arms. But I was smaller than a Ken doll. And they didn't have their bike headlights on.

Side by side, they came rocketing down the middle of the street. They were talking loudly, laughing, pedaling like crazy.

I tried to run. Too late. They were practically on top of me.

I hit the pavement. Dropped to my stomach on the hard asphalt. Shut my eyes and tried to squeeze my arms and legs in as tight as I could.

I could feel a heavy bike tire scrape past me. A burst of wind swept over my body as the bikes sped by.

It took only a few seconds, but it seemed like an hour. My whole body shook as I pulled myself to my feet.

A close call. I watched the two bikes disappear around the corner.

I made it to Ava's house without any other problems. As I stepped up to her front door, I was shaking and sweaty and smelly and dirty. But mainly, I felt angry.

How could she DO this to me?

Ava's family has a cat door at the bottom of their front door. So it was easy for me to slip inside.

The front hall was brightly lit. The house was warm and smelled of dinner. Chicken, maybe.

Creeping down the hall, I glimpsed Ava's parents in the kitchen. They were clearing the dinner table. Dinner was over. I figured Ava must be in her room.

Luckily, the Munroe house is all on one level. No upstairs. No stairs for me to climb.

Keeping an eye out for their cat, I hurried down the hall to Ava's room. It was at the end of the back hall. I stepped inside and gazed around.

Ava likes bright colors. Her walls were red and green. Like they were decorated for Christmas. A woolly red rug covered the floor.

She had posters of her favorite music stars up and down every wall. The posters covered almost all the space between the floor and the ceiling.

Her collection of stuffed sheep jammed the bookshelves in one corner. Dozens of round black sheep eyes stared out at me as I made my way to the bright green table she used as a desk.

Ava was leaning over her laptop, typing furiously. She didn't even notice the curtains blowing wildly in front of the open window in front of her. She wore a yellow T-shirt and white tennis shorts. She was barefoot.

The light from the screen made her blue eyes glow. She was biting her bottom lip, concentrating hard on what she was writing.

I stepped up beside the leg of her chair. "Ava?" I shouted up at her. "It's me!"

She kept typing. She brushed back her blond hair with one hand and kept typing with the other.

"Ava?" I cupped my hands around my mouth to make my voice louder. "Look down! It's me! Down here! Ava?"

She kept typing. She couldn't hear my tiny voice.

I had no choice. I had to get her attention.

I moved forward and wrapped my arms around her bare leg. I hugged her leg tight.

She let out a deafening scream.

Did she think I was a bug? Or a rat?

Her foot flew up. I fell to the floor.

And she slammed her foot down hard to squash me.

22

"Huh?"

I heard Ava gasp.

The big foot came to a stop inches above my head.

I was sprawled on my back on the red carpet. Ava's face floated into view.

Her blue eyes bulged in shock. Her mouth dropped open.

I sat up. "Ava? It's me!" I called up to her.

"Steven?" She blinked several times. "No. It can't be."

"Ava—" I started. "You have to listen to me. I—"

"Is this one of your magic tricks?" she demanded. "How are you doing this? Is this some kind of video projection?"

"It's me!" I cried. "Ava, I shrunk."

"No no no no!" She pressed her hands against her cheeks. Her mouth was twisted in horror. "This isn't happening. No way."

She reached down and grabbed me around the waist. "Oh, no. You're real."

"I'm trying to tell you—"

"How are you doing this, Steven?" she cried. "Tell me right now. Tell me how you are doing this. You are totally freaking me out."

"*You're* freaked out?" I shouted. "What about *me*? I'm the one who is freaked out, Ava. You did this to me. You and Courtney."

"Are you *crazy*?" she cried. She tightened her fingers around me and lifted me off the floor. She swung me up and sat me down on the edge of her green table.

Her blue eyes narrowed as she studied me. She poked me in the stomach with a pointer finger. "I . . . don't believe this," she murmured. "Steven, it's really you? You really shrank?"

"I—I—I—" I sputtered. "Stop poking me! I'm not a doll."

She lowered her gaze. "Where did you get those black plastic shoes? And—and . . . what are you wearing, Steven? *Doll* clothes?"

I swung a fist in the air. "Ava, I swear, if you laugh at me, I'll *kill* you!"

She laughed. "Steven, you couldn't kill a *flea*!"

"STOP LAUGHING!" I shrieked.

She stopped. "Sorry. It isn't funny. It's . . . frightening."

"Yes. Frightening," I agreed. "I don't think

you're listening to me, Ava. It's your fault. It's totally your fault."

She squinted hard at me. She brought her face closer. Her head was as big as my whole body. "My fault? Why are you saying that? How could it be my fault?"

"That drink you and Courtney g-gave me," I stammered. "It shrunk me. You did it. You gave me those chemicals, and they shrunk me."

"But, Steven—" she started.

"You've got to help me," I said. "Tell me what those chemicals were. Tell me what I drank. Maybe a doctor will know an antidote. Maybe—"

"Steven, listen—" She brought her face closer.

"Just tell me!" I screamed. "What was in that drink? *Tell me!*"

She sighed. "Okay, okay. Stop screaming like that. I—I'll tell you."

23

The window curtains flapped in a strong breeze. I could hear the TV from the den. And I could hear every pounding beat of my heart as I waited for her to speak.

"It was vinegar," she said.

I stared up at her. Her words didn't make any sense to me. It was like she spoke in a foreign language.

She frowned at me. "That's all it was, Steven. Just vinegar."

"Vinegar," I repeated the word. My mind was spinning. "You mean—?"

"Just vinegar and water. No chemicals," Ava said.

"But you said—" I could barely choke the words out. I was totally stunned. "You said you went to the chem lab. You said you mixed up a bunch of chemicals."

Ava shook her head. "You believed me? That was all a lie," she said. "Courtney and I wanted to pay you back for being such a jerk. I wanted to pay you back for dropping those eggs on my head."

"Vinegar," I muttered. "Vinegar."

"That's all it was," Ava said. "No chemicals. Nothing bad. Just vinegar from the bottle in our kitchen."

"Then how did this happen to me?" I cried. "Why did I shrink?"

Ava studied me, thinking hard. "Are you allergic to vinegar?"

"No! No way!" I squeaked. "I'm not allergic to vinegar! Ava—look at me. I'm, like, six inches tall. I'm wearing doll clothes. That's not an allergy. An allergy doesn't shrink you down to the size of a chipmunk!"

"Okay, okay." Ava clamped her hands over her ears. "Stop screaming. Your squeaky voice is hurting my ears."

"Well, what am I going to do?" I asked. "What if I start shrinking even more? What if I shrink till I'm out of sight?"

Ava scrunched up her face. "It's weird that you're a magician. I mean, you like to make things disappear. And now you . . . well . . ."

"It's not weird," I said. "It's terrifying. Ava, you've got to help me."

She jumped up. "I'll get my parents. They'll freak when they see you. But they can take you to our doctor. Maybe he can help."

"Thanks," I said. Sitting on the edge of the table, I crossed my arms over my chest.

Ava turned back at the door. "Don't go anywhere," she said. "I'll be right back." She disappeared into the hall.

Don't go anywhere? Was she joking?

Where could I go? I was on top of her desk. The floor was about ten miles beneath me.

I climbed to my feet. I started to pace back and forth across the table. The laptop screen was about my height. The words on the screen looked as big as newspaper headlines.

I walked back and forth, trying to calm down. Mr. and Mrs. Munroe were nice people. They were like family. I knew they would take good care of me. They would contact my parents and —

A strong gust of wind nearly blew me over.

Carried by the wind, the window curtains flew at me. The curtain swept under me. Swept me off my feet.

I tumbled onto my back on the smooth fabric.

And it swung me off the table.

The curtain flew high, carrying me with it.

Another strong burst of wind swung the curtain higher.

I grabbed on to it with both hands.

The curtain flew into the room, then pulled back to the window. Then it swung back out, floated for a while, and swung back.

I held on with all my might. But it was swinging too hard.

The wind battered me. Blew so hard I could barely breathe.

It pushed the curtain and me forward, then back.

My hands slipped.

The curtain swung back to the open window.

I squeezed harder. But my hands ached. My arms throbbed in pain.

I started to slip down the smooth fabric. Struggled to grasp it. Struggled to hold on.

Slipping . . . slipping . . .

I can't hang on!

The curtain flew out the window.

"Whoooooaaaah!" I uttered a hoarse cry as I slid off it and went sailing into the air.

24

I flew into the night sky.

From inside the house, I heard Ava's shout: "Steven? Where are you? Where did you go?"

The wind carried me higher. I heard a loud flapping. Wings?

A heavy blast of air swept over me. A gigantic, feathered head appeared. Two glowing black eyes. A curled beak as big as catcher's mitt.

An owl.

The wings flapped hard as the creature dove toward me. The beak opened. And *snap!*

The bird clamped the back of my jumpsuit collar.

"Hey!" I thrashed my arms and legs helplessly.

The owl made a warbling sound deep in its chest.

The big wings flapped hard above me. I could feel the breeze off them as we started to sail higher.

"Please! Don't drop me! Don't drop me!" I shouted. I shut my eyes and tightened my body, holding perfectly still.

The owl held me prisoner and swooped higher into the night sky.

Where was it taking me? To its nest?

To feed its young?

I sailed high over the rooftops of houses. The street looked like a narrow black ribbon beneath me.

Please don't drop me. Please . . .

The wind battered my face. I dangled in front of the owl, swinging in the stiff gusts.

I crossed my arms tight in front of me. I tensed every muscle.

We flew over my block, then the next.

Please don't drop me. Please . . .

The houses ended in the next block. Deep woods began just past the houses. Dark trees reached up to me as we began to fly lower over the last of the houses.

I knew what was happening. I had guessed right. The owl was taking me to its nest. It had captured its prey. And now it was dinnertime.

I heard a frightening screech.

A dark creature flew toward us. In the dim light, I saw it was another owl.

The intruder swooped at us, opened its beak — and made a grab for me.

It missed.

The round black eyes went wide, as if surprised.

My owl turned and darted lower ... lower ... trying to escape with me, its prey.

The second owl spun in the sky and made another stab. Its open beak jabbed inches from me.

My owl opened its beak and let out a sharp squawk of protest.

And I fell free.

I fell free and dropped like a rock to the grass below.

I landed on my stomach with a hard *thud*. The impact sent my breath whooshing out. I choked and gagged.

Finally, I managed to sit up. I was okay. The fall had been short. The owl had dropped me close to the ground.

But where was I?

I gazed around. The dark woods started to my right. To my left, I saw houses with their lights on.

I swallowed hard. I still felt dazed from the wild flight—and the fall.

I stood up. I gazed at the houses. I recognized the one across the street.

Of course. Of course.

Mr. Pinker's house.

I stared at the yellow light in the front window. The lights were all on.

Yes. My piano teacher's house. *Mr. Pinker must be home*, I realized.

Mr. Pinker will help me.

I started to push through the tall grass toward his house.

How lucky, I thought. The owl had dropped me so close to his house. So close to someone who might help me.

It was my first lucky break of the day.

Now, if I could make it to his house without being grabbed by a worm, or a spider, or a bird, maybe . . . maybe I could get help.

Could I do it?

25

I stared at the glowing yellow light in his windows. They seemed to grow brighter as the night sky darkened.

The street was silent and empty. I darted out from behind a parked car and ran across it as fast as I could.

I kept gazing all around. Gazing up. Gazing down.

I knew that danger could come from anywhere. So I kept alert as I ran up Mr. Pinker's gravel driveway. The gravel seemed as big as boulders, and I kept stumbling and slipping, banging my knees on the sharp edges.

I was surprised to see a pet door down at the bottom of Mr. Pinker's front door. He didn't have a dog or a cat. Maybe the people who lived here before him had a pet. I didn't care, I just wanted to get in.

I took a deep breath and lifted the little metal door. I peeked inside.

The front hall was brightly lit. I saw a stack of sheet music on a table opposite the front closet. I heard music from a back room. Classical music.

The air smelled sweet. I realized Mr. Pinker must have baked another batch of cookies.

I slipped through the door and then stepped into the hallway. Then I tiptoed to the living room. Empty. The piano keyboard cover was down. I saw a stack of CDs on the piano bench.

I started toward the hall. "Mr. Pinker?" My voice came out tiny and high. I knew he couldn't hear me.

I heard a sound. "Mr. Pinker?"

No. Just a creak of the house.

I turned the corner into the back hall. I began walking toward the kitchen.

No. Wait. I'd turned the wrong way.

I stood at the door where I'd glimpsed the tiny dollhouses. The door that Mr. Pinker had chased me away from.

Was he in there?

The door was open a crack. I leaned my shoulder against it and pushed.

It took all my strength to budge the door enough so that I could squeeze inside. The ceiling light was on. I stared at the dollhouses that filled the room.

The houses were taller than me now. Big enough to walk into . . . big enough to *live* in.

I took another step into the room. "Wow." I couldn't believe what I was seeing.

There had to be twenty or thirty little wooden buildings. Narrow roads were painted on the floor. The buildings faced the roads.

They were carefully painted. Most of the roofs were red. I saw white houses with green window shutters. And a gray post office with a tiny flag on a flagpole out front. Next to it—a red firehouse with little fire trucks in the open door.

An entire town. All built of wood and arranged in city blocks.

I moved around the side and saw a market with carts of tiny fruits and vegetables. A butcher store with a pink ham hanging in the window. A gray library with narrow columns in the front.

A row of white and yellow houses had garages at the end of black driveways.

"Totally weird," I muttered. "Why didn't he want me to see this?"

I came closer and looked inside one of the houses.

"NOOOO!" I uttered a gasp of horror.

Through the window, I saw tiny people. Tiny people—about my size—living in the dollhouse!

26

I froze. And stared in shock into the window.

"Who's in there?" I shouted. "Who are you?"

No one moved.

I peered into the house. I could see a boy about my age. He had a round face and straight blond hair.

Behind him, I saw a girl with curly red hair.

"Hey! You in there!" I shouted. "What are you doing in there?"

They both stared straight ahead. Their eyes were glassy. They stood perfectly still. Like zombies.

My heart started to pound. This whole little town was so completely weird. Why did Mr. Pinker build it? Who were these strange kids in that dollhouse?

"Oh, noooo." I uttered a long moan as I stepped closer.

"I'm losing it," I muttered. "Totally losing it."

My mind was so crazed. I was *seeing* things.

I could see clearly now. They weren't kids. They were dolls.

Pinker had dolls in the houses. Boys and girls.

But they were so lifelike. So real.

I stepped up to another house. The roof loomed over my head. I had to go on tiptoe to see inside the open window.

Two dolls—a boy and a girl both in jeans and checkered shirts—were leaning against the back wall. A table held a little tea set.

I stared at the dolls, and a thought flashed into my mind: *Maybe I should trade clothes with that boy doll.*

No. No time, I decided.

I had to find Mr. Pinker.

I couldn't worry about my clothes. Or what this town of dollhouses was doing here.

I was six inches tall. I needed help right away.

I squeezed out of the room, back into the hall. Then I ran to the kitchen.

"Mr. Pinker? Mr. Pinker?"

I found him in the kitchen. He stood over a white counter making balls out of dough and putting them on a big metal baking tray.

The kitchen was hot from the oven. The sweet smell of chocolate filled my nose.

Mr. Pinker had his head bent, concentrating on the cookies. The bright ceiling light made his eyeglasses glow. He wore the gray suit and red necktie he always wore. He didn't even take off his suit jacket to bake cookies!

Classical music poured from a speaker under a cabinet. Mr. Pinker hummed along with the music.

I spotted a blue step stool on the other side of the kitchen cabinet. It had two steps. I pulled myself up onto the first step.

"Mr. Pinker!" I shouted. "It's me — Steven!"

He hummed along to the music as he dropped dough balls onto the cookie tray.

"Mr. Pinker! Mr. Pinker!" I shouted at the top of my lungs. I waved my arms wildly above my head. I jumped up and down on the step stool. "Mr. Pinker! I need help. Can you hear me? Mr. Pinker?"

No. No way. He couldn't hear me over the music and his loud humming.

I pulled myself onto the top step. I waved and jumped and shouted.

I heard a phone ring.

Pinker wiped his hands on a dish towel. The towel looked as big as a bed sheet to me!

He picked up a phone from the counter and began to talk into it. He wedged the phone between his ear and his shoulder. And he contin-ued to drop cookie dough onto the tray.

"Mr. Pinker!" I cupped my hands around my mouth and screamed his name.

I reached up on tiptoe and grabbed the countertop. Using all my strength, I pulled myself up. And scrambled onto the counter.

He had his back turned to me.

I had to get his attention. But how?

I took a deep breath and started to shout again. "Mr. Pinker! Hey, Mr. Pinker!" I jumped up and down and waved my arms frantically above my head.

"Mr. Pinker! Please — Mr. Pinker!"

No. He couldn't hear me over the music from the kitchen speaker. He had the telephone clenched tightly between his shoulder and chin. And he was arguing with someone on the other end.

How could I make him see me? I had an idea.

I jumped onto the cookie tray.

I squeezed carefully through the rows of raw cookies.

"Mr. Pinker! See me now? Mr. Pinker?"

I tripped over a cookie and went facedown on the tray. Two or three globs of cookie dough broke my fall.

I climbed up. I had chocolate and dough stains down the front of my jumpsuit. I rubbed a smear of chocolate off my forehead.

"Mr. Pinker? Mr. Pinker?"

Moving carefully, I made my way to the front of the metal cookie tray.

Pinker had his back turned. He was shouting

into the phone. He was bargaining with someone about buying a piano.

I waved and shouted. He *had* to see me there on the cookie tray.

I took another step toward him—and stopped.

I stared at the cookies all around me on the metal tray. I couldn't take my eyes off them.

The strong aroma of chocolate was making me dizzy.

A wave of cold horror rolled down my body.

I couldn't move. I couldn't breathe.

Why did it take me so long to realize?

How could I have been so stupid?

27

The cookies.

The big chocolate chip cookies. The cookies I was standing in . . .

I ate *two* of them at my piano lesson. And he watched me with such a strange smile on his face.

He watched me eat the cookies with so much excitement. And he didn't take his eyes off me until I had eaten every last crumb.

I thought about how heavy they were. How rich.

I ate TWO of them on the afternoon before I shrank.

What did he put in those cookies?

Some kind of *shrinking* ingredient?

Suddenly, I put it all together. Why didn't I realize?

Mr. Pinker's doll town. The little houses and stores and buildings in his back room.

He didn't want me to see them.

Of *course* he didn't want me to see them.

Because that's where he planned to keep the kids he shrinks. The kids he shrinks with his cookies.

Kids like me.

He planned to keep us in those little houses.

My teeth were chattering. My whole body shuddered. My knees started to fold, and I almost fell off the cookie tray.

Mr. Pinker seemed so kind, so nice.

But it was all an act. An act to trap kids like me.

So we could live with those dolls in his tiny dollhouses?

I had to get away from there.

I couldn't let him see me.

I had to get home. I had to tell my parents about Mr. Pinker and his cookies. I had to show them what he did to me.

I turned and started to the edge of the cookie tray.

My plastic shoe got stuck in a ball of cookie dough.

As I struggled to pull it out, Mr. Pinker reached for the tray.

Then—to my horror—he lifted the tray off the counter.

Still talking into the phone, he swung the tray into the air.

"No, Mr. Pinker! Please—noooo!" I cried.

He didn't hear me. He didn't see me.

He pulled open the oven door.

I felt a blast of heat.

"Mr. Pinker—noooo!"

I gazed around. Could I jump off? No. No way.

Waves of heat rolled over me, burning hot. Burning my face.

Pinker swung the cookie tray down and shoved it into the oven.

28

I shut my eyes. The heat burned my skin. My face felt on fire.

I tried to breathe, but the air burned my nostrils. Burned my throat.

The oven rumbled loudly. A wave of heat knocked me to my knees.

"C-can't . . . breathe. Too . . . hot . . ."

Behind me, I heard a cry.

Mr. Pinker?

The tray shook beneath me. I struggled to keep my balance as the tray began to move again.

Out of the blinding heat of the oven. Into the cool air. The tray swung high. Then it landed gently back on the white kitchen counter.

I wiped the sweat off my face with both hands. I brushed back my soaking wet hair.

And when I could finally see again, I gazed up

at Mr. Pinker staring at me. His eyes bulged and his mouth was wide open. He gaped at me through his owlish glasses.

"Steven? Is it *you*?" he murmured.

"I . . . I . . ." My mouth felt burning hot, so dry I couldn't speak. "Water . . ." I gasped.

He filled a glass with water from the kitchen sink. But the glass was too big for me. He shook his head, thinking hard. Then he returned with a tiny plastic measuring spoon filled with water.

He held it for me, and I lapped up the cool liquid like a dog.

When I finished, he set the plastic spoon down and brought his face close to me. "Steven—how did this happen to you?"

"You *know* how!" I screamed. "Your cookies!"

"Excuse me?" He scratched his fringe of hair. "My cookies? What about my cookies?"

"You—you put something in them!" I cried. "Your cookies made me shrink. You want to put me in that town you built!"

Mr. Pinker squinted down at me. "My cookies? I didn't put anything in the cookies, Steven. They are supermarket cookies."

I gasped. "Huh?"

"They come out of a tube. I get them at the market in the mall," he said. "You just slice the dough and roll them into balls and put them on the baking tray."

I blinked a few times. My heart was pounding. "You don't add anything to them?"

He shook his head. "No. Just slice, roll them, and bake them."

"But—but—" I sputtered. "All those dollhouses."

"It's just a hobby," Mr. Pinker said. "I love building things."

I stared hard at him. He was telling the truth. He didn't shrink me.

I was back where I started. Clueless.

He brought his face down closer to me. "When did this happen to you, Steven?"

"This afternoon," I said. "I did a magic act at school. And when I got home . . . I shrank right out of my clothes."

"Home," Mr. Pinker repeated. "Home. Aren't your parents home? Have they seen you? Have you told them?"

"What time is it?" I asked.

He glanced at the kitchen clock. It was a big copper-colored sun. "It's nearly eight-thirty," he said. "They must be home by now."

I nodded. "Yes. Probably."

"They must be worried about you," Mr. Pinker said.

"They'll worry even more when they see me," I replied.

"I—I'm so sorry," Mr. Pinker said. "I've never seen anything like this—except in movies, of course."

He pulled out a cell phone. "What's your home number?"

I told it to him. He tried it.

"No answer," he said.

Next, we tried their cell numbers. No answer.

"I'll take you home," he said. "We'll wait for them."

He picked me up around the waist and carried me out to his car. He set me down in the passenger seat.

"The seat belt is too big," he said. "Just hold on to the door handle."

I had to reach up to grab the handle.

Mr. Pinker drove to my house very slowly, even though there were no other cars on the street. He kept asking me if I was okay.

How could I answer that question?

I knew maybe I'd never be *okay* again.

He pulled the car up our driveway. Then he carried me to the front door.

He stopped when he saw the two men sitting on the front stoop.

They were both young and dark-haired and had solemn expressions. They both wore white lab coats over white pants. They had small badges pinned to their chests.

They jumped up when we came close. One of them reached for me.

"We've been waiting for you," he said.

29

"I'm Dr. Marcum," the man said. He took me from Mr. Pinker and sat me down in the palm of his hand. "This is Dr. Beach."

"We're from the University Lab for Experimental Research," Dr. Beach said. He had a scratchy, hoarse voice. His dark eyes narrowed as he studied me in the other scientist's palm.

Dr. Beach turned to Mr. Pinker. He fingered the badge on his lab coat. "We're going to take care of this young man," he said. "We have his parents' permission."

Mr. Pinker studied them. "Where are Steven's parents?" he asked.

"They had to go out," Dr. Beach said. "They asked that Dr. Marcum and I take Steven to our lab to make him tall again."

Mr. Pinker shook his head. "I'm sorry," he said. "I can't let you take Steven until I talk to his parents first."

"We are wasting time," Dr. Marcum said. "Every second counts."

"Sorry," Mr. Pinker insisted. "I cannot let you take him."

"You have no choice," Dr. Marcum snapped. He wrapped his fingers around me tightly. And both men started to run toward the street.

Mr. Pinker cried out. He made a wild grab for me.

Dr. Beach stuck out his shoe and tripped Mr. Pinker, who went sprawling onto his stomach on the grass.

Dr. Marcum's fingers gripped me tighter, so tight I could barely breathe.

Their shoes thundered down the front lawn.

They had a white van waiting at the curb. Dr. Marcum shoved me into the backseat and slammed the door.

I heard Mr. Pinker shouting from the lawn. But the two men leaped into the front of the van, and we squealed away.

"Let me go!" I tried to scream, but my voice came out in a tiny, hoarse cry. "Take me home!"

I turned and saw a birdcage beside me on the seat. I peered inside. "Bugsy!"

They had taken the bird, too.

The van squealed around the corner.

"Where are we going? Do you really know how to turn me back to my normal size?" I demanded.

"Yes," both men said at once.

"We'll take you to the lab on campus," Dr. Beach said. "It won't take long."

"But . . . how did you know how to find me?" I asked.

"We saw your dad's ad online," Dr. Beach said. "The ad said you found a missing brown bird. That's our bird."

"We're happy to have him back," Dr. Marcum said. "He escaped from our lab."

"We've been experimenting with birds," Dr. Beach said. "Bugsy is a hawk. He was a gigantic hawk. But we shrank him down to the size of a parrot."

I stared into the front seat. The van hit a bump and I went flying into the air. I landed hard. The cage bounced with me. Bugsy uttered a squawk.

"You—you've been shrinking birds?" I asked.

"We've been testing the effects of Human Growth Hormone," Dr. Marcum explained. "And Human Shrink Hormone. We had great success with this hawk. But then he escaped."

"The bird is dangerous," Dr. Beach said, almost in a whisper. He looked at me. "You see what the bird did to you."

"Huh?" I uttered a sharp cry. "The *bird* did this to me?"

They both nodded. "You must have come in contact with the hawk's tongue," Dr. Marcum said.

"The Shrink Hormone is carried in the bird's saliva," Dr. Beach explained. "I know it sounds crazy. But any contact with the bird's tongue will result in shrinking."

The bird's tongue?

I thought back. I remembered Bugsy nibbling my finger. And then . . . at the talent show. When I made him appear in my act. He — he *kissed* me.

Yes. I remembered the feeling of the bird's scratchy tongue down the side of my face.

And then . . . a few minutes after that . . . I started to shrink.

So *that* was it. Now I finally had the answer. A bird's *tongue* did this to me. How *crazy* was that!?

As we raced down the street, the two men talked quietly to each other. I couldn't hear what they were saying.

A few minutes later, I saw the university campus outside the van window. I saw the green circle surrounded by old brick buildings. Then, a row of campus stores and restaurants.

The van picked up speed and kept going.

"Hey, wait," I shouted. "We went past the campus. I saw it back there."

"Our lab is not really on campus," Dr. Marcum said. "We're almost there."

I knew I couldn't trust them. They had stolen me and Bugsy.

But what could I do? I couldn't escape.

Maybe they WILL return me to normal, I thought. I crossed all my fingers and hoped.

A few minutes later, the van turned off the road and rumbled over a bumpy gravel path. The path wound through some deep woods. We stopped in front of a long, low building hidden far back in the trees.

The building had no sign on the front. It was white stucco with a flat red roof. A row of windows ran down the long front. The windows were small and they were all shut.

"This way," Dr. Marcum said. He lifted me carefully out of the van.

Inside the lab, I heard the screech and squawk of birds. The air smelled sharp and sour.

We walked past a front desk. No one was sitting there. As we made our way deeper into the lab, the bird squawks grew louder. And the sharp odor in the air made my eyes water.

Dr. Marcum carried me down the long aisle, past two rows of birdcages. Some of the cages

113

held flapping birds, all different kinds and colors. Some cages were empty.

"Tell me," I said. "How are you going to turn me back to my old size?"

"We're not," he said.

He opened a cage door. Then he pushed me inside and clamped the door shut.

30

"Let me out of here!" I screamed. "You can't DO this to me!"

Dr. Marcum shook his head and frowned at me. "We can't let you out," he said. "We need to keep you top secret."

I grabbed the cage bars with both hands. "But—but—but—" I sputtered. A wave of panic swept down my body. I struggled to breathe.

"We don't want anyone to know about our secret experiments," he said. "It might scare people."

"But I'm not one of your experiments!" I cried.

He brought his face close to the cage. "You are now," he said. "Don't worry, Steven. We'll feed you and take care of you. Till we figure out what to do with you."

"*Do* with me?" I cried. "You mean . . . you don't know how to make me big again?"

"Not really," he said.

Down the long rows of cages, the birds squawked and flapped. A big yellow bird in the cage beside mine chewed at its cage bars.

"We can try some experiments," Dr. Marcum said. "But we can't let you out."

"But Mr. Pinker knows what you did. And my parents know who you are," I said. "My parents saw you and—"

"Your parents never saw us," Dr. Marcum said. "They weren't home. We broke into your house and took the bird. We saw your clothes on the floor. And the missing doll clothes."

"Then we saw tiny footprints in the soapy water on the floor," Dr. Beach said. "Those little shoes left prints all over the living room. It didn't take us long to figure out somebody had been shrunk. So we waited on the stoop to see who would show up."

I shook the cage bars. "Let me out!" I screamed. "You can't keep me here. Let me out!"

My shouts scared the big bird next to me. He stopped biting his cage bars and began flapping his huge wings hard.

Dr. Marcum turned away and walked down the row of cages.

I shouted after him, but he didn't turn back.

I squeezed the metal cage bars till my hands hurt. My voice was hoarse from shouting. I knew no one could hear me over the caws and chirps and honks of the birds.

I held my hands over my ears. The sound was deafening.

I had to think. But how? I sat down on the cage floor and rested my back against the bars.

How could this happen to me? Here I was a real person, but so small. Sitting in a birdcage. In a lab hidden in the woods on the edge of town.

Did I know a magic trick that would make me disappear from this cage?

No. My tricks were only *tricks*. They weren't going to help me with anything real.

I stood up and started to pace back and forth on the metal cage floor. I stared at the door, which was tightly latched.

This is a birdcage, I thought. *It's made to hold birds inside.*

But I'm not a bird. I'm a person. I know how to work that latch.

All I have to do is push it hard, undo the latch, and the cage door will slide open.

Dr. Beach and Dr. Marcum weren't even good at keeping birds prisoner, I decided. *After all, they let Bugsy escape.*

So, it will be even easier for me to get out of here.

This idea gave me some hope and new energy. I raced to the door and studied the latch. It was just above my head. I had to stand on tiptoe to reach it.

But it was a simple latch, like a hook that caught over a cage bar.

"No problem," I said out loud.

The big bird in the next cage had stopped flapping its yellow wings. It was watching me now. I suddenly realized the bird looked like a canary. But it was huge, as big as a turkey.

I leaned forward and climbed on tiptoe. I reached up and grabbed the latch with my right hand. I pushed.

No. It didn't move.

I pushed harder. No.

I slumped down and took a deep breath. Then I raised myself back up and grabbed the latch with *both* hands.

I pushed. Pushed. Pushed harder, straining every muscle.

No. I couldn't loosen it. I couldn't budge it.

With a sigh I stumbled back from the door. I wiped sweat off my face with the sleeve of my jumpsuit.

Time for Plan B.

But what was Plan B?

31

I gazed at the yellow plastic water dish in the side of the cage. Could I stand on it and try to climb to the top of the cage?

No. No way to escape through the top.

Could I hide in the water dish, then surprise Dr. Marcum or Dr. Beach when they came to find me? And maybe run out while they had the cage door open?

I stepped closer to examine it. No. It was filled with water. Deep enough for me to swim in. I'd done enough swimming in that soapy bucket back home.

I spun around, trying to find something . . . anything. . . .

The giant canary watched me silently as I paced the cage. I turned to it. I took a few steps toward it.

The two scientists must have given it a *lot* of Growth Hormone. It was at least *twenty* times the size of a normal canary.

I studied it for a long while. "You're going to be my magic trick—aren't you?" I said. "You are going to help me escape—aren't you?" I said.

The bird tilted its head as if trying to understand.

"You're going to work some magic," I said softly, gently. "I know you are."

I stepped to the edge of my cage and pressed my cheek up close to its huge orange beak. "Kiss?" I said. "Give me a kiss?"

The yellow bird didn't move. It just stared at me with one round black eye the size of a coat button.

"Kiss?" I pressed my face through the bars. "Come on, birdie. Give me a big, wet kiss."

I gasped as the bird lowered its beak and slurped its wet tongue down my cheek.

32

I swung away from the giant canary. I raised my hand. I touched the wet bird saliva on my skin.

Then I walked to the cage door and waited.

I crossed my arms in front of me and stared straight ahead. And waited for my body to start to feel different.

I waited a minute. Two minutes. Three. I didn't move. I could still feel the touch of the bird's tongue on my skin. Thinking about it made my whole face tingle.

And then I felt a rumbling in my stomach. A sudden ache in my arms and legs.

Was it happening? Was the Growth Hormone from the bird's tongue going to make me bigger?

I stood perfectly still. My knees began to hurt. My toes throbbed.

The jumpsuit felt tight across my chest... around my waist.

Yes!

I started to grow. I could feel myself sliding up. Feel my skin stretch . . . my legs creak . . . my head shoot up.

My head rose to the top of the cage. I nearly filled the cage. Another few seconds and I'd be too big to get out!

I pushed hard against the latch. It popped open. I shoved the door. Swung it all the way out.

I could just barely squeeze out the opening. My arms were stretching. My legs lengthened rapidly. My stomach grew. My feet tore out of the little plastic shoes.

I hit the floor and my jumpsuit made a ripping sound — and flew off.

I stood there, startled. Totally naked. But I didn't care. I was free. And a few seconds later, I stood tall next to the cages. I was my old height again.

Birds squawked and flapped, as if they were celebrating with me.

But I knew I still wasn't safe. I had to get out of that lab. I had to get away from the two scientists.

Over the squawk of the birds, I heard their voices far down the hall. The exit to the lab seemed a mile away.

How could I distract them and get out the door?

Only one way. I began moving down the row, opening cage doors. I pulled and prodded the birds out of their cages.

They came flying out, eager to be free. Birds of all sizes. Birds that had been shrunk. Little birds that had been stretched into giants.

Cages toppled and crashed to the floor as I moved down the row. Birds flapped and flew and soared overhead.

Dr. Beach and Dr. Marcum came running into the aisle. They shouted angrily as birds rushed at their heads. The two men frantically grabbed at birds, trying to capture them and return them to their cages.

They were surrounded by escaped birds. Screaming and cursing and swinging their hands furiously, the two men didn't even see me as I darted past.

I reached the exit and hurtled outside. I left the door wide open. Birds flew out and soared toward the sky.

I took off, running down the gravel path in my bare feet. Behind me, I could hear the men's angry shouts over the deafening bird cries.

I watched to see if they were coming after me. But no. They were too busy with their escaped birds.

How did I get home? It was all a dark blur to me.

I ran all the way. I kept away from the roads. I tried to stay behind hedges and trees. I ran through backyards.

It was a dark night, no moon or stars. I don't know if anyone saw me, a naked twelve-year-old boy running as hard as he could.

Mom and Dad were so happy to see me. Of course, they had a million questions for me. I said, "I'll tell you everything. Just let me get some clothes on!"

I can't tell you how happy I was when my jeans and T-shirt *fit*!

At the dinner table, I told Mom and Dad everything, from the beginning. Dad called the police to tell them about the two men and their science lab in the woods.

Then I settled down to my favorite dessert. Chocolate ice cream with chocolate syrup over it.

The spoon felt good in my hand. It was the right size.

I was the right size. The *world* was the right size again.

The chocolate ice cream was helping to calm me down. All three of us had big smiles on our faces.

Then I heard a flapping sound at the window.

I gasped as Bugsy came flying in. Mom and Dad cried out in surprise.

The bird fluttered over the dining room table.

"He—he followed me home!" I stammered.

And then Bugsy landed on my shoulder. His claws dug into my T-shirt.

He leaned his beak forward.

"No!" I cried. "No, Bugsy! Don't kiss! Don't kiss! Bugsy! Oh, nooooo!" I wailed. "He *kissed* me!"

WELCOME BACK TO
THE HALL OF HORRORS

Well, Steven, that's quite a tall tale you told me. Or should I call it a *short story*?

Here. Let me pick you up and carry you to your room for the night. Whoa. Are you putting on weight? You must weigh at least two pounds.

Tonight you will sleep in the guest deadroom. I have a comfy dresser drawer made up for you.

Don't be afraid. There are no birds flying around in the Hall of Horrors.

Well . . . only vultures.

I am the Story-Keeper, and I will keep your story here where it belongs.

But now I'm being rude. We have a new guest.

Come right in, young woman. Don't be afraid of my pet scorpions. They only sting when they haven't been fed for a while.

Hmmmm . . . Have I fed them recently? I don't remember.

What is your name, dear? Monica? I see you are carrying a Halloween mask. A very ugly, frightening mask. Does this mean you have a Halloween story for me?

Come in. Plenty of room in the Hall of Horrors. You know ... There's Always Room for One More Scream.

Ready for More?

Here's another tale from the Hall of Horrors:

THE FIVE MASKS OF DR. SCREEM

My brother, Peter, tightened the belt around his white karate uniform. "Monica," he said, "if you get more Snickers bars than me, can we trade?"

He didn't wait for me to answer.

"Mom, are we allowed to eat unwrapped candy?" he shouted. Mom was downstairs. How did he expect her to hear him?

He did a little dance and gave me a hard karate chop on the shoulder.

"*Ow.* Stop it, Peter," I groaned. I rubbed my shoulder.

He laughed. "You're such a wimp." He pretended to chop me again. I ducked away.

"Can you get dizzy from eating chocolate?" Peter asked. "Freddy Milner says if you eat enough chocolate, you get so dizzy, you can't walk straight."

"Don't try it tonight," I said.

He staggered around the room till he crashed into the wall. Then he leaped in the air and did a high karate kick.

"Look out!" I screamed. He almost kicked my laptop off the desk.

"Why don't you get out of my room and wait downstairs?" I said.

"Why don't you make me?" he said. He grinned his toothy grin as he raised both fists.

Peter thinks he's cute, but he isn't. For one thing, he's too tall to be cute. He's ten — two years younger than me — but he's nearly a foot taller than I am. He has stringy blond hair and a long, bent nose and funny teeth. He's my brother but let's face facts — he's a beast.

He picked up a postage stamp from my desk. Licked it — and stuck it to my forehead. Then he collapsed laughing on my bed.

"Why did you do that?" I growled.

He shrugged. "Why not?"

Guess you can understand why I spell Peter's name P-A-I-N.

He talks too much. He can't stand still. He's always dancing and chopping and kicking. And he thinks he's funny, but he isn't.

My friends can't stand him.

Some kids take pills to slow them down to normal speed. But my parents make excuses for Peter. They say he's just high energy.

Like I'm some kind of lazy slob. I'm only captain of the gymnastics team and star sprinter of the Hillcrest Middle School track team.

"What kind of costume is that?" Peter asked

with a sneer. "A pair of black shorts over purple tights?"

"It's my gymnastics uniform," I said.

He laughed. "You look like a freak."

"Mom!" I shouted down the stairs. "Do I have to take him?"

I heard her footsteps on the stairs. I stepped out into the hall. She stopped halfway up and leaned on the banister.

"Monica, are you still complaining?" She blew back a strand of her curly copper-colored hair.

She and I have the same color hair. Actually, we kind of look like sisters. We're both small and thin. Unlike Peter and Dad, both gangly hulks.

I sighed. "I just want to meet up with Caroline and Regina and hang out with them."

"Well, you can't," Mom said. "You have to take Peter trick-or-treating."

I rolled my eyes. "But, Mom, all he does is practice karate on us till we're black and blue."

That made Peter laugh. Behind me in my room, he picked up one of my stuffed pandas and gave it some hard chops.

"You girls can defend yourselves," Mom said. "Kick him back."

Peter dropped the panda to the floor. "Huh?"

"Besides, he'll be too busy collecting candy," Mom said. "You know he's a total candy nut. He won't have time to pester you and your friends."

She shouted to Peter. "Am I right?"

"Whatever," Peter replied.

I sighed again. "Okay, let's get it over with," I said.

I returned to my room and pulled a silvery mask over my eyes. Maybe people wouldn't recognize me. The elastic band caught in my hair. As if being with my brother wasn't enough pain.

I turned and saw Peter pull a black mask down over his eyes. It matched the black belt around his uniform. Peter is nowhere near a black belt. But he wears one anyway.

A few seconds later, we stepped out the front door. Peter hopped down the steps and went running to the street.

It was a dark October night. A half-moon hung low over the houses across the street. The wind gusted, making dead leaves swirl in circles in the front yard.

I shivered. Maybe my shorts and tights and sleeveless T-shirt were a mistake. Maybe I needed a jacket.

But as I followed Peter away from the light of the house into the blue-black darkness, I realized I wasn't shivering from the wind.

Normally, I'm not a fraidy cat. But I just had a feeling . . .

. . . A very bad feeling about this Halloween.

Caroline wore a top hat, a ragged man's over-coat, big floppy shoes, and a bumpy rubber nose. She spoke in a high, creaky voice and said she was a Munchkin from *The Wizard of Oz.*

Regina wore gray spandex workout clothes. She had black whiskers painted on her cheeks. She said she was Catwoman. With her olive-colored eyes, she looked like a cat even without the whiskers.

All three of us are on the gymnastics team at school. So we are pretty strong and athletic.

But we were no match for Peter.

He kept dancing around us, making wide circles. Then he'd dart in and snatch something out of our trick-or-treat bags. He was a total thief.

"Give that back!" Regina cried. She made a grab for the candy bar Peter swiped. "That's my favorite!"

"Mine, too," Peter said, dancing away, giggling

his head off. He shoved Regina's candy into his big shopping bag.

Regina didn't give up easily. She let out a roar and dove at Peter.

He dodged to the side and gave her a hard karate chop — in the neck.

"*Ullllp.*" Regina made a horrible noise and started to choke.

For once, Peter stopped dancing. "Oh. Sorry," he said. "That was an accident."

"*This* is an accident, too!" Caroline cried. She lowered her shoulder and plowed right into Peter.

The two of them went rolling into a pile of dry leaves. Peter held on to his trick-or-treat bag for dear life. He swung it at Caroline, and she rolled away from him.

Regina rubbed her throat. "I'm okay," she said.

"It was an accident. Really," Peter insisted. He jumped up and trotted over to Regina. He held up his shopping bag. "Take a candy. Go ahead. Take any one."

Regina eyed him suspiciously.

He shook the bag in front of her. She reached in and pulled out a big Snickers bar.

"Not *that* one!" Peter cried. He grabbed it out of her hand and backed away with it.

Regina let out a groan. "You creep!"

Caroline took Regina by the arm and started to pull her away. "Catch you later, Monica," she called.

"Hey, wait —" I started after them. "Where are you going?"

"Away from the Karate Monster," Caroline said. "*Far* away."

My two friends took off, running hand in hand down the sidewalk. I watched them appear and disappear in the circles of light from the streetlamps.

Then I turned angrily to my brother. "Thanks for chasing my friends away," I snapped.

He shrugged. "Can I help it if they're losers?"

I wanted to punch his lights out. But we're a nonviolent family. I mean, everyone but Peter.

So I just swung my fists in the air and counted to ten.

"Okay." I felt a little less angry. "Let's go home." I started to walk, but Peter grabbed my shoulder and spun me around.

"We can't go home, Monica. It's too early. And look —" He shook his big shopping bag so I could hear the candy rattling around inside it. "My bag is only half full."

I laughed. "You're kidding, right? You really think you're going to fill that *huge* bag? No way. That would take all night."

"Okay, okay," Peter replied. "Just one more block. Two more blocks. Three —"

I rolled my eyes. "One more block, Peter. But you can do both sides of the street."

"Okay. Stand back. Here goes." He ran full speed up the front lawn to a brightly lit house with a big grinning jack-o'-lantern in the front window. A flickering candle inside it made its jagged eyes glow.

I stayed at the curb and watched him ring the doorbell. A girl in a Dora the Explorer costume appeared at the door.

Shivering, I hugged myself. The wind had grown colder. It felt heavy and damp, as if it might snow. The half-moon had disappeared behind dark clouds.

It was getting late. I glanced up and down the street. I didn't see any other trick-or-treaters. Peter is such a candy freak. I knew he'd stay out all night if he could.

But I wanted to get home and warm up. And call Regina and Caroline and apologize for Peter for the ten-thousandth time this month.

I stayed down by the curb and watched him run from house to house. This was his biggest night of the year. Bigger than Christmas.

When he got home, he'd turn the shopping bag over on his rug and dump out all the candy. Then he'd sort it for hours, making piles of one candy bar and then another.

He's so totally mental. Sometimes when he was smaller he'd actually roll on his back in his Halloween candy, like a dog.

Of course, that was when he was still cute. Now, he only *thinks* he's cute.

I watched him run up to the last house on the block. It was a tiny square house with two bikes lying on their sides in the front yard. A young woman answered the door and started to hand Peter an apple.

"No way!" he cried. "No apples!" He spun away before she could drop it in his bag. Then he leaped off her front stoop and came running toward me.

"Monica, we have to do one more block," he said breathlessly.

I crossed my arms in front of me. "Peter, you promised," I said. "One last block. That was it."

"But — but —" he sputtered. "Did you see what happened up there? She tried to give me an *apple*! No candy."

I rolled my eyes. "Big tragedy," I said.

"Come on, Monica. Give me a break." He started to pull me across the street.

"It's late," I said. "Mom and Dad will be worried. Do you see anyone else still out here?"

He didn't answer. He tore across the street and started to run along a tall hedge at the corner.

"Peter? Come back here!" I called after him.

But he disappeared into the deep shadow of the hedge.

Where were we? I couldn't read the street sign. The streetlight was really dim. Without any moonlight, it was too dark to see anything.

Tall hedges rose up like black walls. Behind them, high trees whispered and shook.

We never go this far, I told myself. *I don't know this block.*

As my eyes adjusted to the darkness, houses came into focus. Big houses on top of steep, sloping lawns. No lights in the windows. No one moving. No cars on the street.

A sudden howl made my skin prickle.

Was that a cat? Or just the strong wind through the old trees?

I realized my heart was suddenly thudding in my chest. I turned and chased after Peter.

He was halfway up a long driveway that led to an enormous house nearly hidden behind hedges and tall shrubs. The house looked like an old castle, with pointed towers on both sides.

"Peter?" My voice came out in a hoarse whisper.

I trotted to catch up to him. "Let's go home," I said. "This house is totally dark. The *whole block* is totally dark. We've wandered into a weird neighborhood."

He laughed. "You're afraid? Ha-ha. Look at you. Shaking like a baby."

"I — I'm not afraid. But it's creepy," I said. "Let's go. Now. No one is going to answer the door here."

He adjusted the belt on his karate uniform.

Then he straightened the black mask over his eyes. "Let's see," he said.

He pushed the doorbell. I could hear loud chimes inside the house.

Silence.

"See? No one's coming," I said. "Come on, Peter. I'm freezing. And you have plenty of candy. Let's go home."

He ignored me, as usual. He pushed the doorbell again and held it in.

Again, I heard the chimes on the other side of the tall wooden door.

The trees shook in a strong wind gust. Dead leaves blew up against the front stoop, as if trying to get to us.

I heard another howl. Far away. It sounded almost human.

"Peter, please —" I whispered.

And then I heard footsteps. A clicking sound inside the house.

The door squeaked and then slowly slid open. A dark-haired woman in a long dress peered out at us.

Gray light shone behind her. I couldn't see her face clearly. It was hidden in shadow.

"Trick or treat," Peter said.

The woman took a step toward us. I could see her dark eyes go wide.

"Oh, thank goodness!" she cried. "You're here. I *knew* you would come!"

3

She pulled us into her house. I blinked in the shimmering gray light.

We stood in a narrow front entryway. The ceiling was high above our heads. The light came from a huge glass ball dangling on a thick chain above us.

"We — we're just trick-or-treating," Peter stammered.

The woman nodded. Her straight black hair fell over her face. She brushed it back with a pale hand.

I couldn't tell how old she was. Maybe in her thirties, like our parents.

She was pretty, with round, dark eyes, high cheekbones, and a warm smile. Her black dress fell to her ankles, soft and flowy like a nightgown.

"I knew you would come," she repeated.

"What do you mean?" I asked.

She didn't answer. She turned quickly, her long dress swirling around her. And led the way into an enormous, dimly lit front room.

A low fire flickered in a wide stone fireplace on the far wall. It sent long shadows dancing into the room.

Antique black leather couches and armchairs filled the big room.

A tall painting hung over the mantel. It was a portrait of a sad-looking woman in old-fashioned lacy clothes, a single teardrop on one cheek.

Despite the fire, the room was cold. The air felt damp and heavy.

What a totally depressing place, I thought. *Everything is so dark and creepy.*

"My name is Bella," the woman said. She tossed her hair off her forehead with a snap of her head. She stood facing us with her hands at her waist. Her dark eyes moved from Peter to me.

"You are Monica, aren't you?" she said. "And your brother is named Peter."

I felt my throat tighten. "How did you know?" I asked.

"Who are you?" Peter demanded. "Do you know our parents?"

She shook her head. A thin smile spread over her pale, slender face. "You're in the book," she said softly. Her eyes stayed locked on us, as if studying us.

"Book?" I said. "I don't understand."

She leaned a hand against the back of one of the big armchairs. "The book says you would come. It says you will help me tonight."

I glanced at Peter. He rolled his eyes.

Is this woman crazy? I thought.

"We're in a book?" I asked. "You mean, like a phone book?"

Bella shook her head. She motioned for us to follow her. She led us to a library at the back of the living room.

Bookshelves climbed to the ceiling on all four walls. The shelves were filled with old-looking books. The covers were cracked and faded.

Two lamps that looked like torches poked out from high on the walls. The lamps threw yellow light over a long wooden table. Four straight-backed chairs stood around the table.

Blue-black shadows stretched everywhere. I shivered. I had the strange thought that the shadows were *alive.*

Bella reached down to a lower shelf and tugged out a large book. She raised it in both hands and blew dust off the cover.

As she brought it to the table, I saw that the cover was cracked and stained. She held it up so that Peter and I could read the title etched in curly brown letters on the front: *The Hallows Book.*

"Hallows?" I said. "It's . . . like a Halloween book?"

She didn't answer. With a groan, she set the heavy book down on the table. Then she leaned over it, turning the yellowed pages carefully.

"I . . . don't understand," I said. "What is this book?"

"We just came for candy," Peter said. His voice trembled. I could see he didn't like this.

"Read," Bella said. She ran a slender finger down a page. "Come closer, you two. Read what the book says."

Peter and I leaned over the book. It smelled kind of musty, like the closets at Grandma Alice's house. I squinted at the tiny, faded type, and read:

On Halloween night, the doorbell will ring. Two young people will come to Bella's aid. Their names will be Monica and Peter Anderson.

They will be celebrating the rituals of All Hallow's Eve. But Peter and Monica will give up their celebrations. And they will help Bella in her time of need.

I tried to swallow. My throat suddenly felt dry as cotton.

Peter and I stared down at the faded page of the old book. The writing ended there. The rest of the page was blank.

I raised my eyes to Bella.

"This is impossible," I said. "How can this be?"

About the Author

R.L. Stine's books are read all over the world. So far, his books have sold more than 300 million copies, making him one of the most popular children's authors in history. Besides Goosebumps, R.L. Stine has written the teen series Fear Street and the funny series Rotten School, as well as the Mostly Ghostly series, The Nightmare Room series, and the two-book thriller *Dangerous Girls*. R.L. Stine lives in New York with his wife, Jane, and Minnie, his King Charles spaniel. You can learn more about him at www.RLStine.com.

DOUBLE THE FRIGHT ALL AT ONE SITE

www.scholastic.com/goosebumps

FIENDS OF GOOSEBUMPS & GOOSEBUMPS HORRORLAND CAN:

- PLAY GHOULISH GAMES!
- CHAT WITH FELLOW FAN-ATICS!
- WATCH CLIPS FROM SPINE-TINGLING DVDs!
- EXPLORE CLASSIC BOOKS AND NEW TERROR-IFIC TITLES!
- CHECK OUT THE GOOSEBUMPS HORRORLAND VIDEO GAME!
- GET GOOSEBUMPS PHOTOSHOCK FOR THE IPHONE™ OR IPOD TOUCH®!

SCHOLASTIC

GBWE

NEED MORE THRILLS?

Get Goosebumps!

PLAY

Wii — Goosebumps HORRORLAND
PlayStation 2 — Goosebumps HORRORLAND
Nintendo DS — Goosebumps HORRORLAND

WATCH

R.L. STINE — Goosebumps: NIGHT IN TERROR TOWER
Goosebumps: ONE DAY AT HORRORLAND
R.L. STINE — Goosebumps: MONSTER BLOOD

LISTEN

Goosebumps HORRORLAND — THE LIVING DUMMY — STINE — DISC 1 — REVENGE OF THE LIVING DUMMY — R.L. STINE

Goosebumps HORRORLAND — CREEP FROM THE — R.L. — DISC 1 — CREEP FROM THE DEEP — R.L. STINE

■SCHOLASTIC
wwwscholastic.com/goosebumps

THE SCARIEST PLACE ON EARTH!

The Original Bone-Chilling

Series

—with Exclusive Author Interviews!

R. L. Stine's Fright Fest!
Now with Splat Stats and More!

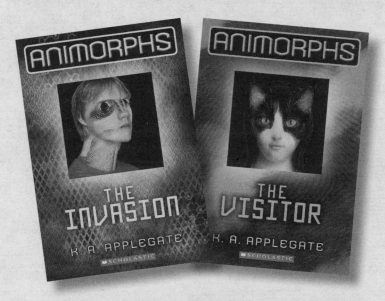

ANIMORPHS™

SAVING THE WORLD WILL CHANGE YOU.

The invasion begins in this action-packed series! Keep reading to discover the fate of the Animorphs.